Raves for the Work of Erle Stanley GARDNER:

"The best selling author of the century…a master storyteller."
— *New York Times*

"Gardner is humorous, astute, curious, inventive— who can top him? No one has yet."
— *Los Angeles Times*

"Erle Stanley Gardner is probably the most widely read of all…authors…His success…undoubtedly lies in the real-life quality of his characters and their problems…"
— *The Atlantic*

"A remarkable discovery…fans will rejoice at another dose of Gardner's unexcelled mastery of pace and an unexpected new taste of his duo's cyanide chemistry."
— *Kirkus Reviews*

"One of the best-selling writers of all time, and certainly one of the best-selling mystery authors ever."
— *Thrilling Detective*

"A treat that no mystery fan will want to miss."
— *Shelf Awareness*

"Zing, zest and zow are the Gardner hallmark. He will keep you reading at a gallop until The End."
— *Dorothy B. Hughes,*
    Mystery Writers of America Grandmaster

NOV – – 2018

"You know something, Donald?" she asked in a low voice.

"What?"

"You're nice," she said. And then suddenly she had her arm around my neck, pulling my head down to the hot circle of her lips. The fingers of her other hand came up and stroked my cheek, then slid around to the back of my neck and tickled the short hairs just above the neckline.

After a moment she broke away. She opened the bathroom door and walked casually out to the studio, saying, "No go, Sylvia. We couldn't raise him."

She turned to me, cool and languid, and said with a casual manner of dismissal, "Well, I guess there's no use, Mr. Lam, I'll let him know that you've recovered the blowgun."

"And are on the trail of the idol," Sylvia Hadley said.

"And are on the trail of the idol," Phyllis Crockett echoed.

I hesitated a moment.

"Well," Phyllis said brightly, "I guess the recess is over, Sylvia. Let's get to work."

Without a word, Sylvia arose lightly from the chair, untied the cord, tossed the robe over the back of the chair, walked up to the modeling platform and resumed her nude pose with the manner of a professional.

"Glad I met you, Miss Hadley," I called. And then couldn't resist adding as I put my hand on the knob of the door, "Hope I get to see more of you."

She smiled at that one...

**OTHER HARD CASE CRIME BOOKS
BY ERLE STANLEY GARDNER:**

THE KNIFE SLIPPED
TOP OF THE HEAP
TURN ON THE HEAT

**SOME OTHER HARD CASE CRIME BOOKS
YOU WILL ENJOY:**

JOYLAND *by Stephen King*
THE COCKTAIL WAITRESS *by James M. Cain*
THE TWENTY-YEAR DEATH *by Ariel S. Winter*
THE SECRET LIVES OF MARRIED WOMEN
by Elissa Wald
ODDS ON *by Michael Crichton writing as John Lange*
BRAINQUAKE *by Samuel Fuller*
EASY DEATH *by Daniel Boyd*
THIEVES FALL OUT *by Gore Vidal*
SO NUDE, SO DEAD *by Ed McBain*
THE GIRL WITH THE DEEP BLUE EYES
by Lawrence Block
PIMP *by Ken Bruen and Jason Starr*
SOHO SINS *by Richard Vine*
SNATCH *by Gregory Mcdonald*
FOREVER AND A DEATH *by Donald E. Westlake*
THE LAST STAND *by Mickey Spillane*
UNDERSTUDY FOR DEATH *by Charles Willeford*
CHARLESGATE CONFIDENTIAL *by Scott Von Doviak*

The COUNT
of 9

by **Erle Stanley Gardner**

WRITING UNDER THE NAME 'A. A. FAIR'

A HARD CASE CRIME NOVEL

A HARD CASE CRIME BOOK
(HCC-136)
First Hard Case Crime edition: October 2018

Published by

Titan Books
A division of Titan Publishing Group Ltd
144 Southwark Street
London SE1 0UP

in collaboration with Winterfall LLC

Copyright © 1958 by Erle Stanley Gardner

Cover painting copyright © 2018 by Robert McGinnis

All rights reserved. No part of this book may be reproduced or transmitted in any form or by any electronic or mechanical means, including photocopying, recording or by any information storage and retrieval system, without the written permission of the publisher, except where permitted by law.

This book is a work of fiction. Names, characters, places, and incidents either are the products of the author's imagination or are used fictitiously, and any resemblance to actual events or persons, living or dead, is entirely coincidental.

Print edition ISBN 978-1-78565-634-7
E-book ISBN 978-1-78565-635-4

Design direction by Max Phillips
www.maxphillips.net

Typeset by Swordsmith Productions

The name "Hard Case Crime" and the Hard Case Crime logo are trademarks of Winterfall LLC. Hard Case Crime books are selected and edited by Charles Ardai.

Printed in the United States of America

Visit us on the web at www.HardCaseCrime.com

THE COUNT OF 9

Foreword

When I try to determine whether my interest in crime comes from writing crime stories, or whether I write crime stories because I am interested in crime, I find I am in the position of trying to find out which came first, the chicken or the egg.

However, the fact remains that I am deeply interested in all branches of crime, crime detection and punishment.

It is in this last field that, in my opinion, society is making its greatest mistake—the mistake of maintaining an attitude of utter indifference.

Whether we like it or not, too many of our prisons are highly efficient factories where weak men become bitter, bitter men become vicious and vicious men become killers.

Some men have their spirit broken so that when they are released they are no good to society or themselves. Some become hardened in the ways of crime. Some are rehabilitated.

Quite obviously, from the viewpoint of society, it would be wise to increase the percentage who are rehabilitated and decrease the percentage who are embittered enemies of society. Statistics show that around ninety-eight percent of prisoners are eventually released. Only about two percent die in prison.

What these men do to society after they get out depends very largely on what society has done to them while they have been in.

All of these things are of enormous importance to the public, yet the general public seems completely unconcerned. If we would pay just a little more attention to the science of penology, if we would listen to our career penologists, if we would try to find out what forces make for rehabilitation and what forces destroy character, we could do a great deal toward cutting down crime.

My friend, Douglas C. Rigg, warden of the Minnesota State Prison at Stillwater, is one of the more forward-looking, modern-thinking present-day penologists. He is deeply concerned over this entire problem of what happens to a man's character after that man is put in prison.

When I last saw Rigg, he embodied his feelings in a few pithy sentences. "If getting tough with these men would cure them," he said, "I'd get tough. If retributive punishment would stop crime, I'd be for it. If I could reform men by punishing them, I'd punish them.

"The trouble is, the problem isn't that simple. There are too many complicating factors and there aren't any easy answers. I know that there are some things which can be done to a man while he is in prison that will tend to rehabilitate him. I know there are some things which can be done that embitter him and build up a hatred of society.

"These men are human beings. Some of them have certain common characteristics, but they are all separate, individual entities. Each one is a problem which must be carefully studied. I would like to see the public take a much greater interest in the problems of penology because I think that interest would pay big dividends."

The August 31, 1957, issue of *The Saturday Evening Post* contains a thought-provoking article by Warden Rigg entitled, "The Penalty Worse Than Death."

Rigg didn't write that article because he wanted the money. He wrote it as one step in a campaign to call to the attention of the public some of the pressing problems of penology.

We need more men like Warden Rigg in the business. There

is nothing soft about him. He can be firm as a rock, hard as steel. He never permits idealism to obscure his practical sense of values. Nevertheless he is a great humanitarian, a great student of the problems of penology, and I wish we had a lot more like him.

And so I dedicate this book to my friend,

DOUGLAS C. RIGG.

Erle Stanley Gardner

Chapter One

As I opened the door and stepped into the reception room, a flash bulb blazed into brilliance and blinded me.

Big Bertha Cool, who had been facing the camera with a fatuous smile on her face, whirled angrily, glared at me and turned to the photographer.

"Did that hurt anything?" she asked.

"I'm afraid it did," the photographer said apologetically. "The opening of the door put it at just the right angle so my flash bulb was reflected back into the camera."

Bertha said, by way of explanation, "It's only my partner." Then, as I hesitated, she said, "Don't worry, Donald. It's just publicity. I have it all fixed up."

She was turning back toward the cameraman when she caught the pose of the filing clerk who was sitting on the corner of the desk with her skirt up over her knees, her toes pointed down so that her crossed legs showed to advantage.

"Now what the hell are *you* doing sitting there sticking that nylon out at the camera?" Bertha asked.

The girl looked helplessly at the photographer.

"She was following instructions," the photographer said.

"Whose?"

"Mine."

"Well, *I'm* the one who gives all the instructions here," Bertha told him. "Any time I want to have a bunch of chippies sitting on the edge of a desk…get your fanny off of that desk. Stand over by the filing case if you want, but don't sit up there with your legs sticking out."

"I'm sorry, Mrs. Cool," the photographer said.

A man who had been standing over behind the filing case came out and said, "We're going to need cheesecake, Mrs. Cool. If we don't have cheesecake, the papers won't publish it."

"Cheesecake in a detective's office!" Bertha Cool snapped.

"Cheesecake in a detective agency," the man repeated stubbornly. "Cheesecake is everywhere. If you don't have cheesecake, you don't get published. There's no use wasting the film on this if it isn't going to make the papers, and if it isn't going to make the papers, Mr. Crockett won't care to employ your agency."

Bertha glowered at him, then said somewhat reluctantly, "This is my partner, Donald Lam—Donald, this is Melvin Otis Olney, who handles public relations for Dean Crockett."

Olney came over and shook hands. "We could have a picture with Mr. Lam and the file clerk," he said. "Lam could be looking for a paper in a hurry, and—"

"Not Donald," Bertha said. "If that girl sticks her legs out in front of Donald, he won't be looking for any paper. He'll be looking at legs....Now let's get that picture."

The filing clerk looked at Olney questioningly.

Olney took the bit in his teeth. "Get back up on the desk," he said. "Get your skirts up over your knees. Don't leave a wrinkle in the skirt as though you had just pulled it up. Try to drape it naturally...here, I'll show you."

He walked over and folded the girl's skirt back, then stood back, surveyed the effect, moved over and draped the skirt down on the side away from the desk.

Bertha glowered at him, with her angry little eyes snapping cold rage.

"Is...is it all right?" the girl asked.

"I suppose it's all right," Bertha said. "If he says he has to have it, go ahead. But you don't need to look up at him with that simpering look while he's feeling your leg."

"He wasn't feeling my leg," the girl said angrily.

"Well, he was getting ready to," Bertha said. "For the love of Mike, let's get this shindig over with so we can get to work."

The photographer, who had replaced the flash bulb and reversed the plateholder, held up the camera. "All ready?"

Melvin Otis Olney said to the filing clerk, "Keep your toes pointed down; both of them. It makes your legs look a lot longer and a lot more graceful. Point them way down. Now take a deep breath....Okay, Lionel, let her go."

Bertha Cool twisted her face into a fatuous smile; a sweetly synthetic grin that was as foreign to her as a postage stamp on a dollar bill.

The flash bulb blazed again.

"All right," Bertha said, "now get the hell—"

"One more," the photographer said, "just as a measure of insurance."

He whipped out another film holder, slammed it into the camera, jerked out the slide, set the shutter, took another flash bulb from his pocket, touched the base of it to the tip of his tongue, inserted it in the socket in front of the reflector, cocked the shutter, held up the camera, and said, "Now smile, please."

Bertha took a deep breath. I could almost hear her teeth grit.

Olney said, "We should have one of the two partners together, and—"

"Shoot it," Bertha said angrily through lips that were twisted into that leering smile. "Somebody's got to work in this joint. Get going."

The photographer waited until Bertha's face returned to just the expression he wanted, his eyes on Bertha's lips.

Bertha, conscious of what he wanted, twisted the corners of her mouth up into a tight-lipped smile.

Once more the flash bulb blazed.

Bertha whirled to the file clerk. "All right," she said, "get off that desk and get back to your job."

Bertha started toward her office, stopped, evidently felt she owed me an explanation, and grudgingly said, "Dean Crockett the Second is giving a big shindig and has retained us to guard the entrance to see that no gate crashers get in.

"The last time he gave a party some gate crashers got away with a jade statue worth six thousand bucks. He wants to make certain that it doesn't happen again. He feels that if we can keep the gate crashers out of the party, the guests who are invited can be trusted."

I said, "You're not to guard the jewelry then, but guard the gates?"

"That's right," Olney said, "the gates—and a little publicity helps, Mr. Lam. Not only helps Mr. Crockett, but helps *me* in *my* job. It helps the agency, and advising gate crashers in advance that they won't be tolerated will be half the battle."

"It'll keep out the amateurs," I told him, "but it just might prove a challenge to some of the more expert ones."

"Well, Mrs. Cool can handle them," Olney said. "That's one reason I wanted her picture for the paper. She looks so decidedly…" He caught himself and said, "Competent."

Bertha glowered at him. "You don't need to pull punches with me," she said. "I'm a tough bitch and I know it."

"We wanted a detective agency that had a woman," Olney explained, "a thoroughly competent woman. Mr. Crockett felt that the last gate crasher who got away with the carved jade statue was a woman. A man can't walk up to a woman and say, 'Pardon me, I think you just dropped a statue down the front of your dress.' A really determined woman is in a different position."

Olney looked at Bertha Cool and smiled.

"I'd have picked her up by her heels, stood her on her head and shaken the damn thing out," Bertha said. "They're not going to get away with anything crude like that when I'm around."

I told Olney I thought it was a smart move, nodded to Bertha and went on into my private office.

Elsie Brand, my secretary, was opening mail.

"How did it happen you didn't get in on the picture?" I asked.

"I wasn't invited."

I looked down at her legs. "You'd have done a lot better job than the filing clerk."

She blushed, then laughed and said, "The filing clerk was acting as receptionist and she was very friendly with the photographer and *very* cooperative. I don't think my legs would have added a thing."

"Two things," I said.

She tactfully pushed the mail at me. "There's one letter that needs to be answered right away, Donald."

Chapter Two

The next afternoon's paper carried the story.

It had turned out to be a pretty good picture. The filing clerk's legs showed to advantage, and Bertha Cool, a hundred and sixty-five pounds of potatoes in a sack, with a bulldog jaw and glittering eyes, was a hard-boiled contrast to the cheesecake. It made a story well calculated to appeal to any wide-awake editor.

There were headlines: DEAN CROCKETT THE SECOND DECLARES WAR ON GATE CRASHERS.

The article gave Crockett quite a build-up; his travels, his big-game hunting, his adventures, his two previous marriages, a picture of his present wife—a sultry combination of eyes and blonde hair on a curved chassis; the penthouse apartment and the story of the gate crashers who got in on the other party. It described Crockett's loss of various trinkets taken by souvenir hunters, and, in particular, the loss of the carved jade Buddha some three weeks earlier.

This party, the article said, was to be guarded by the well-known detective agency of Cool & Lam. Bertha Cool, the senior partner, was going to be on the job personally and woe betide any gate crashers who tried to get in, or anyone who tried to make away with any articles from the priceless collection of Dean Crockett the Second.

The article went on to state that Melvin Otis Olney, Crockett's public relations man and social secretary, had carefully screened the list of guests. It would be necessary, as always, to show invitations before the elevator would go from the top floor to the penthouse.

There would be entertainment by musicians, followed by a showing of the films Crockett had made on his recent trip into the interior of Borneo.

The newspaper article was illustrated not only by the agency picture, but by a photograph of Crockett holding a pygmy blowgun with poisoned darts, and a photograph of his "globe-girdling yacht." It was quite a write-up.

I read the paper and asked Elsie Brand, "How's Bertha taking it?"

"She's a ham," Elsie said. "She's eating it up. She left word to have the papers brought to her as soon as they came out. She's proud as a peacock."

"How about the file clerk?" I asked.

"She has a date tonight with the photographer."

"Fast worker, eh?" I asked.

"Who?" she asked. "The file clerk or the photographer?"

"You think it was both?" I asked.

"Well," she said, "let's put it this way: It was a case of an immovable force meeting an irresistible body."

"I hadn't noticed the irresistible body," I said.

Her eyes lowered demurely. "I don't think you look around as much as you used to, Donald."

"I don't have to," I told her.

Elsie blushed.

"I notice," I said, "that Bertha was quite willing to be the exclusive representative of the firm in the department of public relations. She didn't care about having her partner in the picture."

"On interoffice matters," Elsie Brand said firmly, "I maintain a discreet silence."

"A damn good technique," I said.

"Are you going out to the party, Donald?"

"Not me," I said. "It's Bertha's show. She made the arrangements; she got the publicity; she can stand up there at the elevator and watch the gals go by in the low necklines and peer over once in a while to see if any jade Buddhas are among those present."

Elsie laughed.

I walked down to Bertha Cool's private office, knocked, walked in and said, "Congratulations, Bertha."

"On what?"

"The picture; the publicity."

"Oh…a little publicity now and then doesn't hurt any detective agency."

"That's what I was trying to point out," I said.

Bertha picked up the newspaper which had been opened to the account of the Crockett party and studied the picture carefully.

"Hussy," she said.

"The file clerk?" I asked.

She nodded.

"The public relations man said we had to have cheesecake," I said.

"That's not cheesecake," Bertha snapped. "It's anatomy."

"Well, *you* showed out all right," I said. "You look thoroughly competent."

"I am," Bertha said grimly.

I let it go at that.

Chapter Three

I got in about midnight, showered, crawled into bed and was just turning out the light when the phone rang.

I picked up the phone, said, "Hello," and Bertha Cool's voice came blasting at me like a gust of wind hitting a pile of dry leaves. "Donald," she screamed, "get over here!"

"Where's here?" I asked.

"The penthouse apartment—Dean Crockett the Second."

"What's the matter?"

"Hell's to pay! Don't argue with me!" she screamed. "Get over here. Get the lead out of your pants. Start moving."

"Okay," I told her, "I'll be over."

I dropped the phone into place, got up, dressed and drove over.

I was familiar with the setup from what Bertha had told me and the information which had been in the papers. The entrance was on the twentieth floor of the apartment house. A special elevator had to be taken to reach the penthouse. This elevator ran up and down from the penthouse to a vestibule-like room which opened out from the twentieth-floor hallway.

When Crockett was giving a party, or on special occasions, this vestibule would be open and there would be an operator at the elevator. Otherwise, the elevator was on automatic. Anyone who wanted to see Crockett had to telephone from the desk. If Crockett wanted to see them, he'd have someone come down in the elevator, open the vestibule door and wait for them on the twentieth floor. If he didn't want to see them, there was no way on earth they could get up unless they had a key which fitted the door of the vestibule. Once inside the vestibule, a panel would slide back, disclosing a button which could be pressed and which brought the elevator down to the twentieth floor. Also, if a person knew where to look, there was a concealed panel which slid back to disclose a telephone. This telephone had a direct connection with the Crockett apartment.

The door which opened from the twentieth-floor corridor into the vestibule or anteroom looked exactly like the door to an apartment. It bore the number 20-S.

When I got up to the twentieth floor, the vestibule door was open and an attendant was in the elevator. I gave him my card, but even that didn't do any good. He said, "Wait here," and slid the elevator door shut in my face. Then he went on up and evidently checked with Crockett himself because when he came back down he seemed apologetic as he said, "Sorry, but I was only following instructions. It's all right. I'm to take you up, Mr. Lam."

I got in the elevator and went up.

The door slid back and I was in a reception hallway furnished with Oriental rugs, a crystal chandelier, a line of chairs, and commodious closets, the doors of which could be opened so as to form a private hat and coat checking room.

There was a girl standing behind this checking counter now who wore a skirt reaching to the top of her knees. She looked pretty much beat up. She took my hat and coat and gave me the benefit of a forced smile.

A door opened and Melvin Otis Olney came hurrying out. He was wearing a tuxedo and an expression of abject defeat.

"Come in, please," he said.

"What's happened?" I asked.

"*Please* come in."

I followed him into a room that was furnished with an eye to comfort, but with distinct Oriental overtones.

The people in the room were gathered in a tight little group and it seemed as though everyone was trying to talk at once.

I recognized the tall man in the center of the group as Dean Crockett the Second. His pictures frequently graced the various weekly illustrated magazines, the sporting and hunting magazines, as well as the social columns.

Bertha Cool seemed glad of an opportunity to get away from the group. She came over and grasped my arm, her fingers digging in as though I'd been a life preserver and she had found herself sinking in a hundred feet of water. Her make-up wasn't thick enough to cover the mottled purple hue of the skin. There were little beads of perspiration on her forehead, and she was fighting mad.

"Sonofabitch!" she said.

"Me?" I asked.

"Him," she said.

"That's different," I told her. "What happened?"

She said, "Come over here and I'll tell you."

"Mrs. Cool," Crockett called with a voice like the crack of a whiplash.

"I'll be with you in a minute," Bertha Cool said. "This is my partner. I want a conference with him."

"Bring him over here. I want to meet him—now."

Bertha hesitated, then took me over.

Crockett was a professional he-man.

He stood six-feet-two, with naturally broad shoulders that had been accentuated with padding so as to minimize the waist. He looked like a human triangle.

Looking at him, I remembered a remark that had been attributed to one of his tailors who was reported to have complained, "Hell, the guy doesn't want a tailor. He wants a landscape gardener."

Crockett looked down at me and pushed out a bronzed hand.

The guy made it a business to keep his skin brown. He had sun-bathing for pleasant weather; quartz lamps for cloudy weather, and he kept enough brown on his skin so that when he walked into a restaurant people looked. He wanted people to look.

"So you're Bertha Cool's partner," he said.

He tightened up on his hand and I could all but feel the bones crunch in mine.

"Glad to know you," I said.

"Well, this is a hell of a mess," he told me.

"What happened?"

"Somebody stole the other jade Buddha and my pygmy blow-gun, right under the alert nose of your partner. God knows what else is missing.

"I don't know how much experience you folks have had in this sort of work, but evidently they've pulled the oldest racket in the business. Somebody showed his invitation to the elevator operator, got upstairs, then sent the invitation back down to a gate crasher. The gate crasher used the invitation for the second time and walked right past Bertha Cool. Apparently Mrs. Cool neglected to check off names on the guest list as the guests went up. I'm going to have to take an inventory to find out what's missing, but I know the blowgun is gone and so is the other carved jade Buddha. That's the mate of the one that was taken by a gate crasher the last time.

"My God, I might just as well go in the business of distributing priceless curios like confetti—I didn't feel so bad last time, but this time I'm paying for a guard and I stuck my neck out with all this newspaper publicity. I don't dare notify the police now and have this get in the papers. It would look like hell after the way I had hurled defiance at the potential gate crashers, showing them how I had protected myself against them."

The blonde who came forward had curves, cleavage and courtesy. "Now, Dean," she said, "it wasn't their fault."

"Don't tell me it wasn't their fault," he said. "My God, I paid them money, didn't I? I had this woman standing right there by the doorway inspecting all the invitations. And it turns out she didn't even take the routine precaution of checking off the invitations presented against the name list of the guests."

"When I saw your signature on the invitations that was enough for me," Bertha said.

"Sure, you saw the signature," he said, "but how many times do you suppose you admitted Joe Doakes? It was easy enough for some guy to come up, check in and send his invitation down to a gate crasher who then came back in as Joe Doakes."

"You mean he took the invitation down himself?" I asked.

"Of course not," Crockett said, looking at me witheringly. "He sent it down by one of the caterer's assistants. That sort of thing happens all the time. Someone slips a waiter ten dollars, and the waiter, going back and forth with food and dishes, manages to slip the invitation to the person who is waiting outside with some signal that can't be missed, such as an unlighted cigar in his mouth or something of that sort."

I glanced at Bertha.

Her face was red, her eyes angry. "Well, by God," she said, "they may have slipped a ringer in on me if they doubled up on invitations, but nobody walked past me with any blowgun. I'll tell you that!"

"I feel certain that you'll find the blowgun somewhere, Dean, dear," the blonde said. "You must have placed it somewhere. It would be impossible for anyone to walk out with that."

"My wife," Crockett said shortly, by way of introduction.

The blonde beauty smiled at me.

I remembered she'd been a beauty contest winner some-where before Crockett had married her. She really had what it takes, and she seemed to be a good kid to boot.

"How about that jade Buddha?" Crockett asked. "I suppose you think that was misplaced, too. Somebody smashed that glass case and—"

"I'll agree with you there, Dean," she said, putting a concil-iatory hand on his arm. "But, after all, you can't hold Mrs. Cool responsible for *that*. She was hired only to see that gate crashers didn't get in. If you had wanted her to guard the curios, you should have made it plain that you wanted her to take that responsibility. And then, of course, she'd have had someone up here to keep an eye on things." She flashed me a sultry smile and said, "Her partner, Mr. Lam, perhaps."

Crockett looked down at me again.

Bertha said, "All you had to do was to have told me you wanted that Buddha watched, and it would have been there right now. Donald could have checked the invitations. I'd have stood up there and watched that Buddha, and if any of those babes had tried to slip it down the front of their dresses when I was around, I'd have stripped them to the waist if I had to. But I'd have been damn certain they didn't get away with anything —not while I was watching."

Crockett snorted contemptuously, turned on his heel and strode away.

"You mustn't mind him, really," Mrs. Crockett said. "He's upset, of course, but he'll cool off and forget it. He takes things awfully hard—at first."

"What's the value of the jade Buddha?" I asked.

"Several thousand dollars."

"And the other thing—the blowgun?"

She shrugged her shoulders and the gesture directed attention to the low neckline. "It isn't worth one plugged nickel," she said slowly, and with the emphasis of feeling. "Confidentially, Mr. Lam, I've been waiting for a good opportunity to pitch that thing out of the window. If I could only have been certain I wouldn't have hit some passing pedestrian on the head and hurt somebody, I'd have thrown it out long ago. It's a great long contraption that catches dust, and spiders crawl inside of it whenever you turn your back—Heaven knows how spiders can get into a place like this, but they do. And those darts are downright dangerous. They're tipped with poison and I understand that if a person gets even a scratch from one of those darts it could well prove fatal. I don't dare to let any of the housekeepers do the dusting in his curio room. I have to do it myself.

"Understand," she said, giving me the benefit of a dazzling smile, "I wouldn't want to be quoted on this, but I'll be very, very glad if that pygmy blowgun with the darts never shows up again. I'd like to put an ad in the paper offering a reward—not for its return but to give the person who stole it a bonus."

"Was it jointed or in one piece?" I asked.

"No, it's in one piece. My husband thinks it's a masterpiece of engineering for a primitive tribe to get a limb or small trunk of a tree, or whatever it is, and then get a hole through it that is so absolutely straight—I guess they straighten the limb by fire or steam or something—and then burn a hole through it. Then they must spend hours polishing the inside of that hole. It's a hard wood of some kind, and that hole is just as smooth as glass.

"I've seen Dean put that to his mouth and send a dart through it at such speed and with such force that it's uncanny."

"One of the poisoned darts?" I asked.

"No, no," she said. "He keeps those in a special container; sort of a dark quiver or pouch. But he has made up some darts out of a very light wood...balsa wood, I think it is, and then tipped them with metal and put feathers on the end and wound yarn around the dart so as to make it a tight fit in the blowgun. It's surprising how hard he can shoot them."

"And were those darts stolen?" I asked.

"Those exhibition darts?" she asked. "Heavens, I don't know."

"Where are they?"

"In a drawer in a table in his den. Please don't feel upset about this, Mr. Lam, and please don't pay any attention to what Dean says. He's excitable and he gets all worked up when something like this happens. But I can assure you, by tomorrow he'll be looking at it in an entirely different way—after all, he's had things stolen before. He keeps his curios insured, and when a man gets in his position—well, you just have to expect something like this."

She smiled at Bertha, then impulsively gave me her hand. "You won't feel bad, will you, Mr. Lam?"

"*I* won't feel bad," I said.

"I'll let you in on a secret," she said. "The real reason my husband is so angry is that he hates to lose. He deliberately baited a trap tonight. That's why he's so terribly angry. It also explains why he wanted all that publicity. He was just daring the thief to try and get away with something tonight.

"You see, he's been losing valuable pieces for some time now, and he decided to catch the thief. All this ballyhoo about the detective checking guest invitations was to cover up the fact that he had put in an X-ray elevator."

"An X-ray elevator?" I asked.

"Yes. He put it in two weeks ago. Perhaps you've been in classified defense plants where they put you in a cage and turn on X-rays. A concealed watcher can see right through you, see everything in your pocket, whether you are carrying a gun or a knife."

"I've seen them in prisons," I said.

"Well, every guest who left here tonight was X-rayed. The articles simply couldn't have been taken away...and yet they're missing all right.

"If you'll excuse me, I'll go and pour oil on the troubled waters."

She turned and walked back to join the group in the center of the room, her hips swinging seductively.

"Damn it to hell!" Bertha said to me. "Get your mind off that woman's fanny. We've got to get down to business."

"I am down to business," I said.

"You don't look like it. What the hell are we going to do?"

"It's been done," I said.

"You can't shove this off on *my* shoulders," Bertha said. "It's partnership business—I suppose you were out with some little tart while I was up here watching those goddam guests."

"You didn't ask me to come," I said. "*You* were the one that wanted to be in the pictures. *You* wanted to get the credit. *You* were the hard-boiled babe who was going to grab the women by their heels and shake them until a six-foot blowgun fell out of their bosoms, and—"

"Shut up!" Bertha snapped at me.

"You were standing down by the elevator door, checking invitations?"

"Yes!" she snapped. "And don't ask me why I didn't check them off the guest list or I'll take a swing at you right here in front of all these people."

"That wasn't what I was thinking of," I said. "What about the caterers? How did they come up? Is there a back elevator?"

"No," she said. "There's only the one elevator. Everything had to come up in that elevator, and everything had to go down in that elevator."

"And," I said, "will you kindly tell me how anyone smuggled

out an unjointed five- or six-foot blowgun made of one piece of wood?"

Bertha looked at me and her little glittering eyes blinked rapidly.

"As you told him yourself, you might have slipped up in letting a gate crasher get in," I said, "but I certainly don't think you're dumb enough to stand there and let somebody walk out with a blowgun like that without at least seeing it."

Bertha thought things over, then a slow grin came over her face. "Then it's been hidden," she said. "It still has to be in the penthouse someplace."

"Unless someone heaved it out over the roof."

Bertha said, "He's sent for his insurance agent. I'm supposed to make a statement to him. Boy, I'll be glad when he gets here and I can get the hell out."

"What about the police?"

"Not a word," Bertha said. "He doesn't want anyone to breathe a word to the police. He wants to keep this quiet....What the hell do you do that makes them fall for you like that?"

"What are you talking about?"

"Phyllis Crockett the Second, darling," Bertha said. "She can't take her eyes off of you, and she keeps striking a pose.... My God, I don't know what it is you have. You're a pint-sized little squirt. Dean Crockett could pick you up with one hand. He'd make two of you, and yet—"

"Only one and a half without the padding," I said.

"All right, one and a half without the padding," Bertha said. "But still..." She broke off and looked over at Mrs. Crockett musingly. "And Dean Crockett wears the padding for the family," she said. "There isn't any padding on his wife."

"You want me around for moral support?" I asked Bertha.

"Yes. I want you to talk with the insurance man when he comes. I—this must be the guy now."

The elevator door opened. Melvin Otis Olney escorted a man dressed in a gray business suit. The man looked as though he'd gone to bed, had been aroused from the middle of a sound sleep and told to get over there.

Crockett called us over to the group and introduced us. The insurance man's name was William Andrews. He made notes and asked questions. "How much of a valuation did you place on the jade Buddha?" he asked Crockett.

"Nine thousand," he said, without batting an eye.

"Carved jade?"

"A very high quality of jade," Crockett said. "There's a ruby in the forehead."

"You had a similar jade Buddha stolen a short time ago?" the insurance man asked.

"Yes. This was the mate to that."

"They were alike?"

"Yes."

"In every detail?"

"I tell you, they were a matched pair."

"You put a valuation of seventy-five on the other one," the insurance man said.

Crockett blinked his eyes for a minute, said quickly, "When I said nine thousand dollars, that was a round figure including both the blowgun and the jade Buddha."

"I see," the insurance man said. "Nine thousand dollars for both. That means fifteen hundred for the blowgun."

"And the darts," Crockett said.

"Oh, yes. How many darts?"

"Six."

"Could you estimate how much for the blowgun and how much for the darts?"

"No," Crockett said curtly. "I couldn't. Actually, both articles are priceless. Those darts have a poison that can't be imported into this country—in fact, that whole blowgun outfit is absolutely unique. You can't replace it. It's—"

"I know, I know," the insurance man interrupted. "I was just trying to get a basis of appraisal for the home office, but it's all right. Fifteen hundred for the blowgun and darts; seventy-five for the jade Buddha."

He picked up his briefcase, whipped out a printed form, used the briefcase as a writing desk and started scribbling.

"Oh, never mind doing it tonight," Crockett said, his manner suddenly mollified. "I guess I just got excited. There was really no need for me to have called you, but—"

"No, no," the insurance man said, pausing briefly in his writing to look up with a winning smile. "That's what we're here for; that's the kind of service we try to give.…Here you are, Mr. Crockett. Sign here and we'll have your check in the mail without any further trouble."

Crockett read the claim and signed it. The insurance man opened his briefcase, dropped the claim in, bowed to everyone, said, "Good night…I guess I should say good morning," and started for the elevator.

Bertha seemed somehow stuck on dead center, so I said to Crockett, "Well, I guess there's nothing further we can do."

"The hell there isn't," Crockett said. "I want my stuff back."

I smiled over at Bertha and said, "She's the business manager of the firm."

"What do you mean?" Crockett said.

"I mean," I told him, "that you hired our agency to keep the gate crashers out, not to recover stolen property. If you want to make an arrangement with us to get stolen property back, that's a separate job."

His face flushed and he took a quick step toward me, then paused. His eyes locked with mine and abruptly he laughed.

"Damned if you aren't right," he said. "I guess I owe you an apology, Lam. I had you figured wrong when I met you—I guess I made a mistake."

"Think nothing of it," I told him.

Bertha said proudly, "Lots of people make a mistake about Donald. He's little, but he's tough—and he's brainy as hell."

"Skip it, Bertha," I said.

"Well, I didn't make any mistake about him," Phyllis Crockett said, giving me her hand. "*I* recognize ability when I see it. Good night, Mr. Lam, it was a real pleasure to meet you, and I'm sure my husband will be in tomorrow to discuss business matters with Mrs. Cool."

She turned to Bertha and said, "Good night, Mrs. Cool."

I called out to Melvin Otis Olney, who was piloting the insurance man over to the elevator, "Hold it, Olney, we'll ride down in the elevator with you and that'll save another trip."

"It's all right, I'll hold the elevator," Olney said.

I managed to avoid shaking hands again with Crockett so there was no further opportunity for him to disable my writing hand. We said good night, went to the elevator and the door closed.

The insurance man looked at me, grinned and said, "Take one of my cards—I know your agency but I'd like to have a card, if you don't mind. Just to keep my report straight."

I gave him one of our cards. We got out at the twentieth floor and transferred to an elevator going down to the lobby. Olney took the private elevator back up.

"Do you have much of this?" I asked William Andrews.

"Hell, yes," he said. "I get it all the time. Take some fellow like Dean Crockett. He gets a place packed with curios he's picked up in different parts of the world. By the time he gets back and gets to looking that stuff over, he thinks it's worth a million dollars. We don't even try to talk him into cutting down on his valuation. It's good business. Nobody's going to steal *all* of that junk, but every so often someone picks up a piece that appeals to him, and we pay off at an exaggerated valuation. But our total valuation is so high and the premiums are so high it averages out all right, plenty all right. Everybody's satisfied.

"The only place we could get stuck would be in the event of a fire. But he's in a fireproof building....We're willing to put a million-dollar valuation on that stuff, but if the guy died tomorrow and his estate sold it at auction, you know what they'd get?"

I said nothing, so Andrews tapped the briefcase in which he'd put the claim Crockett had filled out.

"They'd get about ten thousand dollars for the whole shooting works," he said. "That blowgun they'd have to haul off to the junk pile and dump. They'd have to pay hauling charges."

Chapter Four

When I entered the office the next morning, Elsie Brand said, "Bertha is biting her fingernails back to the knuckles."

"What does she want?"

"You."

"Why?"

"This theft at the party."

"I thought she was going to take care of that," I said, grinning. "Newspapers intimated she was in sole charge."

Elsie was usually careful not to discuss partnership affairs, but now she said demurely, "That isn't the way she feels this morning."

"Okay," I said, "I'll go in."

I went to Bertha's private office, went through the formality of tapping on the door, and walked in.

"My God! It's about time you got here," Bertha Cool screamed at me.

"What's the matter now?"

"That damn Buddha and blowgun."

"What about them?"

"We're supposed to get them back."

"He doesn't really want them back," I said. "If he got them back, he'd have to refund nine thousand bucks to the insurance company."

"That isn't the way he talked to me. He wants them back."

"Well, why not get them back then?"

"Don't pull that line with me. How the hell do you go about

getting stuff like that back? Until you joined this agency, I had a respectable run-of-the-mill business, serving papers, making reports, tracing witnesses."

"And making run-of-the-mill money," I reminded her.

"Then you started in working for me, weaseled your way into the business, and we've been playing tag with the state penitentiary ever since."

I looked at her big diamond rings.

Bertha followed my eyes, suddenly grinned. "All right, Donald. I'm out of my depth. How do you deal with something like this without letting the police in on it?"

She pushed her creaking swivel chair back from her desk, got up and started walking back and forth across the office with that peculiar walk of hers which was half-waddle, half-stride. "He had sixty-two guests up there," she said. "Sixty-two. Count them. Sixty-two. All of them with invitations. I checked every damn one of them. All of them, he says, are pillars of respectability...and one of his damn pillars of respectability stole a jade Buddha and a blowgun. Now he wants them back.

"What do you do if you can't call the police? You can't cover pawnshops without calling the police, and that stuff isn't going to show up in a pawnshop, anyway. It's in the private collection of one of those guests...."

"Unless that blowgun is still up there, hidden someplace under a bed or in a closet somewhere," I said.

"Well, it isn't," she told me. "I suggested one of the guests might have hidden it, and they put that whole penthouse through a wringer this morning. They searched every corner of it."

"Try putting an ad in the paper," I said. "Will the person who inadvertently walked out with the curios at a certain party given by a well-known social figure please communicate with Box 420. Reward."

Bertha glared at me. "Don't be facetious."

"I'm not being facetious," I said.

Bertha snorted.

"It's a good, logical suggestion," I told her, "but if you don't want to follow it, you don't have to."

"If *I* don't want to follow it!" she screamed. "You're in this thing! You're the one that's going to have to get that stuff back. I've done my share. I'm not going to carry *all* the load of the partnership business."

I raised my eyebrows.

"I went there and stood on my two aching feet in front of that goddam elevator, being nice to people as they walked in, smiling at them, asking to check their invitations....Don't hand me that line of malarkey, Donald Lam. You're going to take charge of getting these things returned, and I'm going to be busy from now on. When that damn secretary, Melvin Otis Olney, calls, I'm going to tell him you're in charge of that branch of the business."

"How nice," I said, settling down in the chair and lighting a cigarette. "How do you get along with Olney?"

"I hate his guts," Bertha said. "He's a supersmooth, suave, penny-ante, slave-driving sonofabitch!"

"And the photographer?"

"The photographer," she said, "was nice."

"He was there last night?"

"Oh, sure, he was taking pictures all over the place."

"A private photographer?"

"It depends on what you mean by private. Crockett wants pictures. Every time Crockett does anything he wants to be photographed."

"What was the occasion for the shindig?" I asked.

"He's just back from exploring the wilds of Whosis, with a lot of pictures of women carrying baskets on their heads, women naked from the waist up, dead animals with Crockett standing with one foot on the chest of the carcass, his gun resting on his arm and a fatuous smile on his face."

"You didn't see it?"

"I didn't see all of it. I was waiting at the damn elevator until the guests arrived, then I went up and stood by the entrance to the elevator in the upper hall so I could check anybody that came in late."

"Was there anyone?"

"A couple."

"Where was this trip?"

"Someplace down in Africa or Borneo or someplace. I never did give a damn about geography."

"There's a wide distance between Africa and Borneo," I told her.

"And a wide distance between your yakkity-yak and getting that stuff back," Bertha said.

"Any flag planted?" I asked. "The flag of an adventurer's club or something of the sort?"

"Oh, sure," Bertha said. "They all do that. They had motion pictures of the guy sticking the flagpole in the ground, and then they had the flag there, and it was presented to somebody or other with a lot of ceremony."

"And that somebody took it out?"

"That somebody took it out."

"Who was the somebody—do you know?"

"Hell, no. It was some nitwit who was kissing Dean Crockett's fanny all over the joint. He was the manager of some goddam club."

I got up, stretched, yawned, said to Bertha, "Okay, I'll give it a whirl. You don't like my idea of the ad, eh?"

"Get out of here," she said, "before I start throwing things."

I went down for a coffee break and bought a morning paper. Melvin Otis Olney, as a public relations expert, had done a good job. The shindig was written up in style and there were pictures of Dean Crockett the Second, standing with his foot on the chest of some rare animal, pictures of Dean Crockett the Second planting a flag of the International Goodwill Club.

The International Goodwill Club, it seemed, was organized for the purpose of promoting international friendship through dispensing international knowledge of customs, civilization and various cultures of different peoples and races.

I went back up to the office, said to Elsie, "What do you know about our file clerk?"

"Eva Ennis? Not too much."

"How long has she been with us?"

"About six weeks."

"What's her reaction to Bertha?"

"Terrified."

"What's her reaction to me?"

"Wouldn't you rather find out for yourself? After all," she said with dignity, "I'm a secretary, not a procurist."

"Hold everything," I told her. "This is business."

"I can imagine," she said, sniffing.

"Get her in here," I told Elsie, "and just to keep your mind above the belt, you can sit in on the interview."

She looked at me curiously. "What's it all about?"

"Get her in here and you'll find out. I don't terrify her, do I?"

"Apparently not."

"Okay, get her in."

Elsie went out and a short time later came back with Eva Ennis.

I looked Eva over pretty carefully. She had curves, contours and an air of sexual awareness about her that belied the demure expression which was on her face at the moment. She was wearing a high-necked sweater, a jacket and skirt. The sweater was tight.

"You wanted to see me, Mr. Lam?"

"Sit down, Eva," I said. "I want to talk with you."

She smiled at me invitingly, pushed out her chest, then glanced at Elsie.

"Sit down, Elsie," I said. "I want to find out something about Eva's private love life, and I want a chaperone."

Eva started to say something, changed her mind, then blurted out, "I can't imagine a better way to find out about a girl's love life than to have a chaperone."

I nodded as though the remark made sense and said, "I'm trying to get a line on the photographer who was here the other day. I may want to have some work done."

"Oh, Lionel," she said. And then added, "Lionel Palmer."

"What do you know about him?"

"*Really*, Mr. Lam! I only met him day before yesterday."

"That isn't what I asked," I said. "I asked what you knew about him."

"He's nice."

"What does he do?"

"He takes pictures."

"Did he tell you much about his duties?"

"Oh, yes. He travels with Mr. Crockett, and it's up to him to keep a perfect picture record of the trips. He takes color slides to project on the screen in stills, then he takes colored motion pictures, and, in addition to that, he takes black-and-white pictures so there's a perfect story record of all the trips in all three media: color slides, black-and-white pictures, and colored movies."

"Why all the coverage?"

"In lectures Mr. Crockett uses the colored slides. For publicity releases in newspapers he uses the black-and-whites, and for entertainment such as the dinner party last night, he uses colored motion pictures."

"Were you up at the party last night?"

She made a little face, said, "No," shortly and sharply.

"Why not?" I asked. "I thought you were going out with Lionel."

"Who told you that?"

"Come, come, Eva," I said, "let's not be coy. I'm a detective, you know. I saw him, after he was through taking the pictures, pulling out a notebook and jotting down your telephone number."

"My address," she said. "He promised me a print of the picture."

"And he couldn't send it to the office?"

"I wanted it to come to my apartment."

"Did you get the picture?"

"No. I get it tonight."

I grinned and said, "Mail comes in the afternoon. I take it you're getting a special delivery."

Her eyes flashed. "Anything wrong with that?"

"Nothing wrong with that," I said, "but what we were talking about was Lionel. No use being coy. You went out with him last night and you're going out with him tonight."

"I didn't go out with him last night," she said. "We were supposed to go, but there was too much excitement. He had to call me and call it off. He…he was going to fix things so I could slip into the party and see the pictures, and then we were going out for some ham and eggs before he took me home. But they had some excitement up there and he couldn't get away, and I didn't dare to let him try to smuggle me in because…well, you know who was watching the elevator."

"Now we're doing better," I told her. "That's all you know about the situation to date?"

"To date," she said significantly.

"Would it be asking too much to check in tomorrow morning and tell me what else you have found out?"

"What else did you want to know?"

"Something about the guy; what he does. And, in particular, how many pictures he took at that shindig last night. I want prints of all those pictures."

"Why?"

"Because we're working for Mr. Crockett and it's important that I have them. I could get them through Mr. Crockett, but I'd prefer to work with the photographer. I don't like to discuss methods with a client. All I want to do with a client is turn over the results and endorse a check."

She hesitated a moment and the tip of her forefinger traced designs on her skirt at the thigh where it was smoothed tightly over her crossed leg.

"Well?" I asked.

"Okay," she said.

"Fine," I told her.

"Anything else?"

"No."

She got to her feet, started to the door, paused and said, "Understand, Mr. Lam, I'm not a stool pigeon. I...I'm willing to help on anything that's on the up-and-up, but I never double-crossed a friend yet, and I don't intend to."

"No one's asking you to," I told her.

"Thanks," she said, and went out.

Elsie Brand looked at me. "I suppose you know what you're doing."

"Not yet," I told her. "I'm floundering around trying to find out."

"Well, watch that babe," Elsie told me. "I haven't anything to go on except office gossip, but they tell me she has a line of risqué stories in the rest room that are pretty far advanced."

"Thanks for the tip," I said.

Her eyes flashed. "It isn't a tip. It's a warning."

Chapter Five

The International Goodwill Club was listed in the telephone book. I copied the address, went out and got a cab.

I had anticipated the offices would be little more than a mailing address; a hole-in-the-wall place where a part-time secretary could handle mail. I was surprised to find that there was a sumptuous office, back of that a clubroom and a library.

The manager came forward to meet me with a glad hand.

"Lam," I told him, shaking hands. "I'm interested in finding out something about the club. I'm a writer. I want to turn out an article on your club."

"I'm Carl X. Bedford," the glad-hander told me. "I'm secretary and manager. Anything I can do for you, Mr. Lam, I'll be only too glad to do. You see, we are somewhat in the nature of idealists up here and we feel that our objectives are very, very important."

"Nice place you have," I told him.

"It's small," he said. "Our library consists of some rather rare adventure books, geographical magazines and things of that sort. We have a self-service bar; that is, members can keep their own liquor and we have an icebox which makes ice cubes in quantity. We're small but we hope to expand."

I nodded, took a notebook from my pocket, went in and started looking around.

"Specifically, what periodical do you represent?" Bedford asked.

"I'm freelancing," I told him. "I like to get material for articles and then sell them to the best paying market."

"I see." His voice had lost some of its cordiality.

I went around and looked over the books. None of them were new. They had the appearance of having been taken from other libraries. I took down a book at random on Africa, looked at it and found the name of Dean Crockett the Second written on the flyleaf.

"Well, well," I said, "is that the signature of Dean Crockett, the adventurer?"

"Oh, yes. We have quite a number of his books here."

"Indeed."

"Yes. You know the problems of modern housekeeping. Places get smaller and smaller, and there's not nearly as much place for books as…oh, say twenty years ago when persons were living in large houses, or fifty years ago when each well-appointed house had a large library."

"So Crockett donated his books on travel and adventure?"

"Some of them."

"Any other donations?"

"Yes, our members are very generous with donations."

"How many members do you have?"

"Our membership is a very select list. It…well, frankly, Mr. Lam, we cater to quality rather than quantity."

"Could you tell me about how many?"

"I don't think the club would care to publicize the intimate details, Mr. Lam. We'd be very much interested in having something published about the objectives of the club, the promotion of international goodwill, the understanding of foreign culture."

"Well, that's fine. Just how do you go about promoting this understanding?"

"The club puts on a series of lectures throughout the country. We try to get the public interested in the ways of other people, their ideals, their customs, their civilization, their government."

"Very commendable. Do you have paid lecturers?"

"Oh, yes."

"Could you give me their names?"

He hesitated again. "There again it would be somewhat embarrassing to mention specific names. Someone might feel slighted."

"And," I said casually, "I take it the members themselves conduct some of these lectures."

"Oh, yes. That's a very important part of our program."

I turned to look at him. "Specifically," I said, "are there any lecturers who you can call to mind who are not members of the club?"

"No, I think not. You see, the matter is one of such extreme delicacy that the club wants absolute accuracy. Therefore, it doesn't dare to take chances with someone who may have a gift of gab but who is lacking in accurate information."

"You have a club flag?"

"Yes, indeed we do."

"I take it you have some flags that have been planted in unusual parts of the world?"

"Indeed we have, Mr. Lam. We have a wonderful collection of photographs showing some of the expeditions on which the club pennant or flag has been taken."

"If I get an article, could I get some of those photographs with which to illustrate it?"

"Oh, yes. I'm quite sure you could. We'd be only too glad to let you have some of them."

"Do you have scrapbooks available?"

"Indeed we do, Mr. Lam. Here is a whole shelf of them."

He slid back a panel and showed me two full shelves of scrapbooks.

I picked one at random. It was a trip made by Dean Crockett the Second to Africa.

I pulled down another one. It contained photographs of a tiger hunt in India. Another one had big-game hunting in Alaska.

"Nice photographs," I said.

"Yes, aren't they."

"How about seeing some of the flags themselves. Do you have them here?"

"Oh, yes, we have them in a closet—a special closet."

He opened a door and pulled out a long sliding rack which glided smoothly on rollers. There were probably two dozen flags with engraved semicircular plates screwed into the handles, telling the name of the member of the club, the expedition on which the flag had been planted.

I went through the flags. The same names kept repeating themselves. There were twenty-six flags and five different names.

"This last one in the rack," I said casually, "is the most recent expedition?"

"That's right," he said. "That flag was presented to me only last night by Dean Crockett the Second. It was planted in the wilds of Borneo, a most remarkable expedition."

I lifted the flag out of the rack, then I lifted out the flag next to it which had also been planted by Crockett in the rugged barranca country of Mexico.

I shook both flags up and down. The barranca flag was solid. Something jiggled and banged in the handle of the Borneo flag.

"Well, well, what's this?" I said. I put the barranca flag back in the rack, turned up the Borneo flag and looked at the bottom. There was a metallic screw cap on the bottom.

"Oh, that," Bedford said, laughing. "That's a concession to utility, Mr. Lam. You see, there's an interchangeable point which screws on the bottom of the flag. When a flag is being planted, the explorer screws on this pointed piece of metal. It is very sharp, very hard, very smooth. It's quite easy to plant the flag in the ground, then it is photographed and there are appropriate ceremonies. Afterward, when the explorer brings the flag home, it would be exceedingly awkward to have a point like that on the flagpole. So we have it so the pointed tip can be unscrewed and this blunt point is screwed into place. That prevents any accidents, and, of course, makes it much easier to store the flag here in the closet."

"Nice going," I said, and unscrewed the metallic cap, put it in my pocket and tilted the flagpole.

A long, black piece of wood started sliding out.

I pulled it out with my hand and said, "What's this?"

"Well, for Heaven's sake," Bedford said, "that...why, that is a blowgun...that looks exactly like...like...why, that looks like Mr. Crockett's blowgun! Now what in the world would *that* be doing in here?"

"That's the point," I said. "What in the world would it be doing in there?"

It was well over five feet long, of a black, hard wood that was like iron. It had been heated, rubbed and polished until the thing looked like metal. I tilted it up to the light, and the interior of the blowgun was a smooth, polished tube as brilliant as glass.

I stood the blowgun in the corner against the racks, screwed the cap back on the flagpole, which was now much lighter than the other flags, and put the flag back in the rack. I picked up the blowgun and said, "Well, thanks a lot for the interview."

"Here, wait a minute," Bedford said. "Where do you think you're going with that blowgun?"

"Eventually," I said, "I'm going to return it to its owner."

"How do you know who the owner is?"

"I know the same way you do. It's Crockett's blowgun."

"Well, I'll do the returning, Mr. Lam. That happens to be club property."

I smiled at him and said, "*I'll* return it."

He came forward and stood hulking over me. "The hell you will!" he said, his eyes angry. "Give me that blowgun."

I said, "You can probably take it away from me, but when you do, I'll step over to that phone and call the police."

"I don't think Mr. Crockett would want any publicity about it."

"The way for Mr. Crockett to avoid publicity," I said, "is to have me return the blowgun and you keep your mouth shut."

"What do you mean by that crack?"

I said, "That blowgun was stolen. I'm commissioned to recover it.. That's why I came here in the first place."

"You...you—"

I took out a leather folder and showed him my card certifying that I was a duly licensed private detective.

"Satisfied?" I asked.

He kept batting his eyes. "You're a detective?"

"Yes."

"I...I never would have thought it."

I didn't say anything.

"You had me fooled."

"Perhaps you'd like to tell me how it happened that you took that blowgun from Crockett's penthouse last night."

"I didn't take it."

I grinned at him, a sort of knowing leer that I thought the occasion called for.

"I assure you, Mr. Lam, that I know nothing of it. I was presented with the flag as the secretary of the club, and I took the flag to have it properly inscribed with a brass nameplate and placed in the rack."

"Why don't you and I have a nice little talk?" I said.

"What do you mean, a talk?"

"You wouldn't like to have this racket exposed, would you?"

"What do you mean, a racket?"

"Ever show your books to the income tax department?" I asked.

"Certainly not. Why should we?"

"You're a profit-making corporation."

"Indeed we are not, Mr. Lam. We're incorporated as a non-profit corporation for the purpose of promoting international goodwill and understanding."

I grinned at him. "That last is what I really wanted to know."

"What last?"

"That you're incorporated as a nonprofit corporation. Now, *I'll* tell *you* what happens. You've got a membership list of eight or ten individuals; probably no more than that. You have a lot of honorary members who are nothing more or less than suckers. Your active members donate large sums of money to the club. The club, in turn, finances their expenses when they go on trips.

"Take Dean Crockett, for instance. He wants to go to Borneo. He has his yacht, his photographer, his public relations man, his wife and four or five guests. If he went there and charged it as a pleasure expedition, the expense would be prohibitive even for a man of his wealth. By the time he paid the expenses and then earned enough to pay those expenses, and then paid income tax on the money he'd spent on the trip, he'd be broke.

"But he makes a donation to the club of fifty thousand dollars, then the club turns around and sponsors an expedition by Crockett to Borneo. Crockett comes back and gives the club a flag, and a duplicate print of colored motion pictures taken on the trip. He also has his photographer prepare a scrapbook dealing with the trip, and that is filed in the archives of the club. He submits an expense account, fifty thousand, six hundred and seven dollars.

"Crockett doesn't report getting expenses of the trip as income because the club simply paid his expenses. On the other hand, he does report the fifty-thousand-dollar donation to the club as being a tax-exempt donation.

"In that way, a group of millionaire members manage to take their hunting trips, keep their yachts up and take their friends around the world all on a tax-deductible basis.

"I even suppose that the shindig Dean Crockett gave last night for his friends was termed a lecture on behalf of international goodwill, trying to promote an understanding between the social elite of this city and the savage tribes of Borneo. You'll be paying the caterer's bill, and Crockett will make a donation to cover."

Bedford looked at me with consternation stamped all over his face. "Who...who are you working for?"

"Right at the moment I'm working for Dean Crockett."

"Well, you don't act like it."

"The hell I don't," I told him. "I'm working for the guy on a special mission. I was hired to get the blowgun back. I've got it.

"All this other stuff I'm telling you I'm throwing in gratuitously to impress upon you that you don't want to monkey with me because if you do, this whole racket is going to get in the newspapers. And if the racket gets in the newspapers, you'd lose a very soft job."

He stood there blinking that over.

"Good morning, Mr. Bedford," I said, taking the blowgun.

He took in a deep breath. "Good morning, Mr. Lam," he said, bowing formally.

I walked out, taking the blowgun with me.

Chapter Six

The address of Lionel Palmer was in a district of cheaper type, obsolete office buildings. These had, at one time, housed respectable and perhaps pretentious offices, but now were given over to lofts, rooms for garment cutting and alteration, and a few mail-order businesses.

As I opened the door marked *Lionel Palmer—Photographer—Entrance*, a bell on the door sounded in back somewhere. An electric sign flashed on which read, "Photographer is busy in darkroom. Will join you in a moment. Please sit down and wait."

I looked around.

There was a desk, a swivel chair, a couple of straight-backed chairs, a studio camera, some stock backgrounds, and a shelf of portable hand cameras. This shelf was protected by a sliding glass cover.

There were some framed camera portraits and quite a few enlargements of hunting scenes, in each of which Dean Crockett the Second was very much in evidence.

It took about two minutes for Palmer to come out. His eyes were blinking in the light. "I'm sorry I kept you waiting," he said. "I was in the darkroom loading some plateholders, and... well, well, well, it's the detective."

"That's right."

I got up and shook hands.

"What are you doing here? I mean, is there something I can do for you?"

"I'm leading a double life," I told him.

"That's nothing," he said. "Double lives are simple. It's triple and quadruple lives that give you the excitement. What do you want?"

"Pictures."

"What of?"

"The shindig last night."

"I'm making some of them now," he said.

"I want to study the pictures," I said.

He frowned for a moment, then said, "Okay, I'll treat you as one of the family. Come on in."

The darkroom had been constructed so that by means of an S-shaped labyrinth the outer light was kept from the darkroom. It was a big darkroom. An orange light showed the pin-up pictures.

The walls were literally covered with pin-ups; some of them were artistic nudes; some of them were just naked women; some of them were a more daring type of cheesecake than any magazine would publish. There were no pictures in the place except those of women. The only ones who had more clothes on than could be covered by a couple of good-sized postage stamps were the ones who were doing the high kicks or those standing over a wind machine in a house of fun.

"Quite a collection," I said, looking around and whistling.

"I get around," Palmer admitted.

"I want prints of your shindig pictures," I told him.

"What for?"

"So I can study the faces of the people who were there."

"You're working for Crockett, Lam?"

"That's right."

"You think these pictures will help you recover the stolen articles?"

"They may."

"That would be nice for you."

"In what way?"

"You'd get a reward?"

"No one's said so—not yet. My partner makes the financial arrangements."

"I'd be helping you cut yourself a piece of cake?"

"I wouldn't know."

"If I help you, perhaps you could help me."

"Perhaps."

"I happen to be awfully short of cash right now," he said. "Hang it! I can't ever seem to keep money ahead. I want to take a babe to dinner tonight."

"Have you been making passes at that file clerk in the office?" I asked.

"What office?"

"Ours."

"Oh, that babe." He took a book out of his pocket, switched on a brighter light, ran through the book and said, "Let's see, what was her name? Oh, yes, Ennis. Eva Ennis. Here's her telephone number."

"That book looks well filled," I said.

He riffled through it, shrugged his shoulders and said, "After I've been out with a babe three or four times I get fed up. I like to play the field and get new ones."

I said, "I'd like to talk babes, but I've got to get the pictures of that shindig last night. You took lots of flash-shots?"

"About fifty."

"Any I can look at now?"

"No extra prints yet," he said, "but you can look. That's what I've been doing today, developing the negatives and pulling some eight-by-ten enlargements on glossy. They're just coming out of the dryer now. Want to look?"

"Sure."

He manipulated a big drum covered with canvas. I heard

prints dropping, then the canvas slid back and I saw a big heated, stainless-steel drum, polished to a mirror finish.

Palmer opened a drawer and the prints came out; some three dozen of them.

"That's nice work," I told him.

"I do nice work."

"They feel nice."

"Double weight paper," he said, "and I soak it in a glycerin bath after I've washed the hypo out of them and before I put them on the drum dryer."

I started looking through the prints. "Some nice-looking babes here," I said.

"Uh-huh."

"You know their names?"

"I can find out their names. Each one of these is numbered. I number the plate when I take a picture, and then I get names in a book reading from left to right."

"Addresses?"

"That depends. Some of them want prints; some of them don't care."

"Crockett gives them the prints?"

"I do. Crockett wants the pictures. I tell them they have to make arrangements with me."

"What sort of arrangements?" I asked.

He winked at me and said, "It depends on the age."

He put his fingers on a photograph, indicating the cleavage of an attractive young woman who was leaning over as the picture was taken. "This babe likes pictures," he said. "She's a nut on pictures....Know what I think? I think she's going to try to crash the movies or TV, and she wants some nice pictures. She asked me to take some professional shots a while back. Want to look?"

"Sure."

He opened another drawer, took out the usual eight-by-ten professional portraits, then some full-length shots with legs and bathing suit.

"Nice looker," I said.

He hesitated a moment, then took an envelope out of the drawer. "You look like a good egg," he said. "Maybe you'd be interested in these."

I opened the envelope. It had half a dozen five-by-seven shots of the same girl. This time she was posing for pictures I was certain had been suggested by the photographer. Clothes were absent.

"How do you like that number?"

"Class," I said.

"Lots of them are like that. I won't monkey with them unless they're real class."

He stood looking at the nudes thoughtfully. Suddenly he threw back his head and laughed.

"Know how I got this babe, Lam?"

"How?"

"This is one I invented myself, and, boy, is it a scream."

I stood there waiting.

"You've been out at the airport and seen these machines where you get a hundred and twenty-five thousand accident insurance in lots of twelve thousand, five hundred to twenty-five thousand at a throw?"

I nodded.

"Okay," he said. "You go out with a babe, don't make any passes at her unless she makes them at you, play her along, keep her guessing a bit. Then go down to the airport, put two bits in a machine and take out a policy in her name. You get a carbon copy that you put in an envelope and mail to her."

"Then what?"

"Forget the whole business," he said. "A week or so later you call her up. She wants to see you. She's puzzled as hell. She says, 'How did it happen that I got this insurance policy?'

"You look at her and brush it off. You say, 'Oh, what the hell? I was taking an airplane trip, I saw this insurance machine and somehow I had a hunch maybe this time was going to be it.' Then you laugh and say, 'It was a bum hunch. It didn't pay off.'

"But the babe is looking at you sort of funny-like. She says, 'All right, you had the hunch, but how did it happen you put *my* name on the policy?'

"Right there, of course, is the place where you've got to watch carefully that you don't go too far and get sucked into buying an engagement ring. You start talking fast. You tell her that she may not realize it, but there's something that she has that makes quite an impression on a guy; a little trick she has of smiling, the way she walks, and so on. And the first thing you know, you've got her going.

"You know, so many guys make the mistake with a babe by trying to turn on *their* charm and hypnotizing the jane. The thing to do is to tell the frail how much charm *she* has and how she can certainly make a man reach for his hole card. From there on, *she's* the one who's trying to make the sale—you know what I mean? No babe likes to think she can't make a big smoke.

"So you wait until she's pretty well extended and then you move in for the kill, and that's all there is to it."

"Well, I'll be darned," I said thoughtfully. "What the hell—and you thought that up all by yourself?"

"Sure. I've got lots of them. A guy that has tastes like I have wants to get around and wants company. I'll tell you another good stunt if you're in a strange town."

"What's that?"

"Go into a telephone booth at the airport and start looking

through the directory. Now, here's something you may not have realized: a guy gets into town, he has a babe staked out and he's in a hurry. Fellows who travel by air are the kind who don't waste time. While they're waiting for their baggage to come out, they go into the telephone booth and make a call.

"Now here's what happens: the light usually isn't too good in those booths out by the incoming baggage. A man will hold the directory up so he gets the light on the name he wants. Then he'll take a pencil and make a little dot opposite the name, or maybe just a small check mark. In that way, if the line is busy on the first try, he can drop his dime, then look down at the number and dial right from the book."

"And those numbers are all live?" I asked.

"Hell no," he said. "Some of them are the names of boyhood friends; some of them are business numbers. But some of them are babes who are on the make.

"You use your own judgment. If the number is E. L. Lewiston, that's one thing, but if the listing is Evelyn L. Lewiston, that's a pretty good bet.

"So you drop a dime and give it a try. A girl's voice answers and you start making. You tell her, 'I'll bet you don't remember me. The last time I saw you, I was with somebody else. You were on a date with the other guy and I couldn't even make a play for my babe because I couldn't take my eyes off you.'"

"Then what?"

"If she isn't that kind, she gets dignified and tells you you've got the wrong number. But if she's the type you're looking for, she's interested. She starts trying to remember when and where, and you get cagey and tell her you don't want to offend your friend who had her out, but you made up your mind you were going to call and see what the chances were of speaking for yourself, John.

"Hell, there's a dozen different approaches. You can just sit out there and sometimes make them up off the top of your hat."

"I don't think that fast," I said.

"You do when you get a babe on the line. You can always tell her that you remember what the other girl said about her. A babe may or may not want to know what *you* look like, but she sure as hell wants to know what the other girl was telling around about her. That's a line that *never* misses."

"God," I said, in awe, "do you know women!"

"Do I know women," he admitted. "Say, I don't know why I got started telling you all the tricks; but you pick out the pictures you want, and I'll get some babes lined up and we'll have a date. Meanwhile I've got some work to do. You can sit out in the office and go through the stuff."

He fixed me up at the desk, gave me a bunch of scrapbooks and said, "I'm going in and load some more plate-holders, then I've got some stuff in the hypo I want to take out and wash. Just come on in whenever you've got your stuff lined up. Look in these scrapbooks. Those photos are all first-class babes."

I thanked him and sat down at the desk.

After he'd gone back to the darkroom, I started exploring the office. I looked at the array of cameras on the shelf and picked out the press camera he'd been using in the agency office. It was a Speed Graphic. I opened the back. There was nothing in the camera. I looked in the backs of a couple of other cameras and figured I'd drawn a blank. I guessed I'd have to suffer through a date with the guy and a couple of his babes in order to get the lead I wanted.

Then I saw another Speed Graphic with a wide-angle lens.

I swung that around and opened the back. It was in there: a carved jade Buddha about four inches high, all wrapped in cotton. There was a big flaming ruby in the forehead.

I put the statue in my pocket, ran through the enlargements and the scrapbooks. I chose some prints of the shindig, went into the darkroom and said, "Here's a list of the pictures I want."

He took the list, said, "That's swell. I'll make prints tomorrow. Did you find any frails you liked in the stag book?"

"I liked 'em all. You sure can pick 'em."

"Where do we meet tonight?" he asked.

"Just a minute," I told him. "I'll have to get a clearance from the office."

I dialed the office and said, "This is Donald Lam talking. Where's my secretary? Is she around?"

"Just a minute," the operator said.

A moment later Elsie Brand came on the line and said, "What is it, Donald?"

I said, "Look, I'm playing around with a little romance tonight. Any reason why I can't go out on a heavy date with another guy and a couple of broads?"

Elsie's voice was cold as ice. "I know of no reason," she said.

"Wait a minute!" I yelled at her. "Don't hang up. Go and ask Bertha."

"Bertha isn't in," she said.

"I'll wait," I said.

There was a moment of puzzled silence at the other end of the line, then Elsie Brand hung up.

I held the dead phone for a couple of minutes, then said, "Hello, Bertha. I've got something lined up for tonight, and—" I broke off and let my face show dismay.

After a minute, I said, "Now look, Bertha, this is something special. I—"

After a while I tried it again. "Look, Bertha, this is business. This really is. This guy is someone who has some contacts with…with a client of ours. I want to—"

After a few seconds, I said wearily, "Okay, if that's the way it is. Okay, okay, quit yelling. I'll take over on the damn thing."

I slammed the telephone disgustedly into the cradle and shook my head at Lionel Palmer. "Tied up," I told him. "That's the hell of this business."

His face showed disappointment. "Gee, I was looking forward to something swell tonight."

"And I wanted to get some lessons," I told him. "I'd sure like to learn some of the stuff you know about women."

"Hang around me and I'll show you the works," he said. "You look like a good egg."

We shook hands and I went out.

Chapter Seven

I walked into my office. Elsie Brand nodded coolly.

I closed the door, said, "Now look, sister, next time I cut you in on a deal, at least follow suit and don't start trumping my aces."

"What do you mean?"

"You know damn well what I mean!" I told her. "If I had a heavy date, I wouldn't be asking you for permission to keep it. When I ring you up with some kind of a stall that way, at least stay on the line and start playing along until you can find out what I'm after. For all you knew, that conversation might have been monitored. As it was, I had to keep talking to beat hell after you had slammed up the phone so I could get out of a date I didn't want to keep."

Her face lit up. "Oh, I'm sorry, Donald. I didn't know what it was you had in mind."

"Next time," I said, "have a little more confidence in me. Stick around and try to see what I'm shooting at."

I went over to my closet, opened it and took out the blowgun.

"Would you mind telling me what that is?" Elsie asked. "I went in there to hang up my coat and—that's the darnedest-looking thing I ever saw."

"That," I said, "is the nucleus of a juicy little fee....Is Bertha in?"

"She's in."

"Alone?"

"I think so. Want me to ring?"

"It's all right," I told her. "I'll go on in."

I took the blowgun and walked into Bertha's office.

Bertha was pouring words into a dictating machine; her voice high-pitched and metallic.

She looked up in annoyance, shut off the dictating machine, said, "Damn it, when I want you, I can't ever find you. But when I'm right in the middle of an important letter you—Donald, what the hell is *that*?"

"That," I said, "is the missing blowgun."

I reached in my pocket and took out the jade Buddha. "This," I said, "is the missing jade Buddha.

"Since you've had the personal contact with Dean Crockett the Second, it might be a good plan for you to return the loot."

Bertha looked at me with her double chin resting on her Adam's apple; her little piggish eyes were big and wide for once. "What the hell!" she said.

I stood the blowgun in the corner, brushed a little imaginary lint off my coat sleeve, said, "Well, I'll be getting along...."

"Come back here, you bastard!" Bertha Cool screamed at me.

I stopped and looked over my shoulder in surprise.

"Something else?" I asked.

"Something else. Where the hell did you get those things?"

"From the people that had stolen them."

Bertha Cool's diamonds flashed in a scintillating arc as she pointed a finger at a chair and said, "You park your fanny right there in that chair and tell me what the hell this is all about."

It isn't often you can take Bertha like that. It made me feel good.

I sat down and lit a cigarette while Bertha's glittering eyes were fastened on me, getting more angry by the minute.

"Any old time," Bertha said. "I've got all the rest of the afternoon—what there is of it."

"Well," I said, "you were standing by the elevator watching

people as they went in, watching people as they went out. The blowgun was over five feet long. You'd have to be pretty dumb to let somebody walk by you carrying a five-foot blowgun."

"You mean it hadn't been taken out at all?" she asked.

"No," I said, "it was taken out. It must have been taken out. The place was searched and there wasn't any blowgun. It either was taken out or thrown off the roof. And there was no indication it had been thrown off the roof."

"Go ahead," Bertha said.

"So," I told her, "it was only necessary to look around for something that could be taken out of the place without exciting attention, something that would hold a blowgun over five feet long. Once you started thinking along those lines, it wasn't at all difficult."

"Where was it?"

"In the pole of that club flag that the secretary took out."

"Then *he* stole it?"

"I don't think so."

"He's the one who took it out."

"Sure, he's the one who took it out," I said, "but I doubt if he knew the blowgun was in there."

"Why?"

"Well, in the first place," I said, "the job had to be carefully engineered. The poles on those flags are made so they can be driven deep into hard ground. They're made of sturdy wood. Now, somebody who knew the exact dimensions of this blowgun had to take that club flag and bore a hole in the pole, or have a hole bored in the pole. You can't do that just on the spur of the moment. In the first place, it is a delicate job and a high precision job. And in the next place, it would leave shavings, sawdust and litter."

"You mean it was done outside of the penthouse?"

"Done outside of the penthouse well in advance and cut to very careful measurements."

"I'll be a dirty name," Bertha said. "Fry me for an oyster.... Who do you think planned the whole thing?"

I shrugged my shoulders. "We were paid to get the loot back."

"How about this Buddha?" Bertha asked.

"The Buddha was simple."

"Yeah, I know," Bertha said, with grudging, unwilling admiration in her voice. "You just got a list of the guests, walked to the guest who had taken the thing and said, 'Give it back,' and that's all there was to it."

"Actually," I said, "it was even simpler than that."

"What do you mean?"

"We knew," I said, "that the inside of the private elevator going to the penthouse was equipped with X-rays just like these booths you stand in before you go into some of the state prisons. Whenever anyone left the penthouse apartment, he was standing right in front of an X-ray machine for a few seconds; long enough for the watcher with a fluoroscope on the back of the elevator to get a complete inventory.

"You knew that, I knew it, and, presumably, the person who was going to take the jade Buddha knew it—but no jade Buddha showed up in the X-ray machine. Therefore, it didn't go down in the elevator—at least in the ordinary manner."

"What do you mean, in the ordinary manner?"

"I mean the person who went down with that idol wasn't X-rayed."

"Why not?"

"Because he was one person who couldn't be X-rayed. There must have been an arrangement to shut off the X-ray when this one person went down. I could think of only one person who would have had that arrangement."

"Who?"

"The photographer. He was carrying cameras and films in and out. An X-ray would have fogged the films. Since the pictures of the banquet shindig weren't fogged, it's a cinch the photographic equipment wasn't X-rayed—either in or out."

Bertha blinked her eyes, adjusting to that. "And the photographer had it?"

"It was concealed in his equipment. We'll put it that way."

"What did he say when you got it?"

"He doesn't know I have it. I stole it from him."

"Fry me for an oyster!" Bertha said.

I got up and walked out.

Chapter Eight

Elsie Brand showed me a clipping from the paper. "Seen this?" she asked.

It was a gossip column with a lot of news about persons in the public eye, a lot of veiled insinuations which probably had been made up out of the columnist's head, such as: "What contractor is living in a fool's paradise, ignorant of the fact that his wife has had private detectives trailing him for two months now and knows all about that apartment up on Nob Hill...? How does it happen that whenever a certain lawyer, whose last name begins with M, always finds night work for his secretary it's on the Wednesday evening when his wife is attending her club meeting...?"

"What about it?" I asked Elsie.

She placed the tip of her finger on a paragraph near the bottom: "It is rumored that a wealthy individual who spends much of his time cruising around in foreign countries, getting material for a tax-exempt foundation, has been away from home too much, too often and too frequently. His much younger wife has other plans for spending the rest of her life."

"Is that supposed to mean something to me?" I asked.

"It should," she said.

I was about to say something when Bertha Cool appeared in the doorway, standing militantly with the dark wood blowgun in one hand, the jade Buddha in the other.

"Don't think I'm going to go parading up there with this junk," she said.

"You're going to fix the fee, aren't you?"

"You're damn right I am."

"Then you'd better have the last contact with the client."

"The last contact," Bertha said, "will be when I fix the fee. I'm not going to do it in his house, going up there like a delivery boy.

"I've been thinking this thing over. Donald, you have to admit that when it comes to financial matters, Bertha has the right hunches....Now, here's the way to play this. You take this stuff up and deliver it. You tell him about how you recovered it. Don't make it look so damn simple and easy, the way you did when you were telling it to me.

"Dress it up a bit. Tell him about the way you reasoned things out, only don't tell him that you started in the middle of the book. Go back to first principles. Tell him about casing the joint so as to determine there really was only one elevator. Dress it up."

"He may resent that," I said.

"He can resent it and be damned. We have a living to make. He's already put a value on that bunch of junk at nine thousand bucks. We've got it back for him without any fuss or trouble."

I shook my head and said, "Nix, Bertha, nix."

"What the hell do you mean, nix? I'm talking about money."

"I'm talking about money, too," I told her. "But let's be logical about it. If it had taken a month to grab this stuff, we could have built it up into a big play. The way it is, we went out and grabbed it.

"We can't possibly build that up into a big job without getting in trouble with questions of business ethics and all of that. Therefore, since it's got to be a relatively small job anyway, why not minimize the thing and make it appear we toss those things off every day before breakfast?

"We send him a bill for the work of one operative for one

day, and dress it out a little with expenses in the line of taxi fares, meals and incidentals. We get in solid with a new client. The next time Crockett has any job, we're in on it. Any time Crockett's friends want anything done, they'll come to us because they'll have heard all about us from Crockett."

Bertha blinked her eyes and said, "I'll think it over. I'll sleep on it before I send him a bill. You *may* have a point."

"I know I have a point."

"All right, Donald, you take the junk up there."

I said. "If you promise to make the guy a nominal charge, I'll take the stuff over and give him a build-up on the work."

"It's a go," Bertha said, and literally shoved the stuff into my hands.

"Want me to telephone and tell him you're coming?" Elsie Brand asked.

I hesitated for a moment, then grinned and said, "No, I want to see the guy's face when I hand him the stuff. That hole couldn't have been bored in the flagpole without *somebody* in the house knowing about it—in other words, that had to be an inside job. I want to find out whether Dean Crockett the Second carefully arranged to have this stuff missing and then called us in as window dressing, and, if he did, why he did it."

"Don't get tough with him," Bertha warned.

"I won't unless I see a blazed trail leading to where I want to go," I told her.

"How about the photographer? Couldn't he have done the whole thing?" Bertha asked.

"He might have," I told her, "but I have another idea on that."

"What?"

"I'm not certain the photographer even knew the idol was in the camera."

"Why?"

"The way it was wrapped in cotton."

"What does that have to do with it?"

I said, "Suppose some woman wanted that idol and knew that the best way to get it out of there was to conceal it in a camera. That Speed Graphic that the idol was in had a wide-angle lens. In other words, it was a one-shot camera. The photographer used that to take a picture of the guests at the table, and then that was the last shot he was going to make with it that night.

"Anybody that knew the photographer and knew cameras could be pretty certain of that, so that was the camera in which to hide the jade idol.

"So some woman who wanted that idol used Lionel Palmer as a cat's-paw to get the chestnut out of the fire for her. Then she intended to come drifting into Palmer's studio to make an appointment, ask some question or perhaps to keep a date with Palmer, who is about the most obnoxious type of hound you can imagine. She watches for an opportunity, opens the back of the camera, slips out the idol and that's that."

"What about the cotton?" Bertha asked.

"That's what makes me think the photographer didn't do it."

"Go on," Bertha said.

"The cotton was just pushed in there loose. Loose threads of cotton can stick to the inside of a camera and raise merry hell with photographs. A photographer might have put a soft cloth inside the camera, but he wouldn't have been apt to have packed the idol in loose cotton and then put it in the camera."

Bertha's greedy little eyes lit up. "Look," she said, "I've got an idea. Tell him that for the moment you can't tell him where you recovered the idol because you're working on it to try and fix the responsibility. That'll give us four or five days' more work. You can hang around that photographer's studio and see who comes in."

"I couldn't hang round that guy for a week without killing him," I told her.

"Then *I'll* cultivate him," Bertha announced. "It's an idea we can develop. Then we can make a complete report to Crockett and tell him whether his photographer should be fired or whether the guy is a tool."

"You try hanging around him," I told her, "and you'll learn about the facts of life."

"I know the facts of life," Bertha said.

"You'll learn ramifications, variations."

"I've been ramified, verified and mutated," she said. "Get the hell out of here. You go make a build-up with Crockett, and I'll take on the job of turning this photographer inside out…or maybe we could get Eva Ennis to do it. I notice he fell for her."

I shook my head and said, "You're all wet, Bertha. The thing to do is to put the cards on the table with Crockett, make a quick turn on the thing, and then if he wants any additional information about Lionel Palmer, he'll give us the job of finding out."

Bertha sighed wearily. "Arguing with you," she said, "is as bad as trying to argue with the calendar. Get the hell out of here and do it your way. You're going to, anyway."

Chapter Nine

I couldn't get past the guy at the desk in the apartment house without telling him where I was going—that damn blowgun.

If I had been able to walk in there as though I owned the place, I could have at least taken a chance at bulling my way past the desk. But that blowgun made me stand out like a sore thumb.

"You'll have to be announced," the man said.

"Donald Lam," I said, "calling on Mr. Crockett."

He relayed a message upstairs, said, "Mr. Lam, Mr. Crockett is not available at the moment, but his wife will see you in her studio. It's on the twentieth floor, on the other side of the building. I'll have a boy take you up."

"Okay," I said.

Come to think of it, no one was going to surprise any expression on the face of Dean Crockett the Second. The guy had himself surrounded with too many fences. He wasn't going to be surprised—period.

A boy rode up to the twentieth floor with me, then, instead of going toward the place where the secret elevator went to the penthouse, he detoured me down a corridor and pushed the chimes on Apartment 20-A.

Mrs. Crockett came to the door, all smiling and gracious. She was wearing a painter's smock and smelled a little of turpentine.

She saw what I was carrying and her face lost its smile. An expression of shocked amazement came into her eyes.

"The blowgun!" she said.

"The blowgun," I said. And added, "I also have—"

"Mr. Lam. do come in."

She dismissed the bellboy with a smile and I entered the apartment.

"This is my hobby," she said, by way of explanation. "This is where I spend a good deal of my time. I love to paint, and my husband is away so much, you know. I have a good deal of time."

She glanced at me mischievously. "And they do say as how the devil finds mischief for idle hands."

"So you are afraid to have yours idle?" I asked.

"Not afraid," she said. "I think it's better that way." Then she looked at me again and said, "They're not idle all the time. Come into my painting room."

The apartment had evidently been specially designed for a studio. There were panes of frosted glass reaching high and on an angle. There were drapes so that the light could be controlled. There was an easel, a canvas on it, dozens of canvases around the room, and a nude model standing on a dais in a position somewhat resembling the female figures which for a while were put on cars.

"Oh, I forgot about you," Phyllis Crockett said. "I...but I guess you won't mind."

"Well, it's pretty late to voice an objection if I did," the model said.

Phyllis Crockett laughed. "I daresay Mr. Lam has seen nudes before."

She walked over to a chair, looked around and said, "Where's that robe of yours, Sylvia? I—"

"I hung it in the closet after I took it off."

"I'll get it," Mrs. Crockett said, "and then I'll present you formally."

The girl laughed and said, "Oh, go ahead, present me and *then* I'll get the wrap."

Phyllis said, "Miss Hadley, this is Donald Lam. He's been working on a job for…well, he has some things to leave for Dean."

Sylvia Hadley smiled at me, said, "Pleased to meet you, Mr. Lam."

She walked calmly over to the closet.

She slipped a robe over her shoulders, walked over and sat down.

That was the first time I took a good look at her face. It was the face of the girl whose photographs I had seen in Lionel Palmer's studio earlier in the day.

Suddenly an idea hit me between the eyes.

"You have the blowgun and the—" Mrs. Crockett asked.

"The blowgun," I said firmly, interrupting her.

"Oh, I thought you said you had the—"

"The blowgun," I interrupted again, smiling. "The other part of the job is, I think, showing progress, but…" I turned to the model and said, "You're a professional model, I take it, Miss Hadley?"

She shook her head and smiled.

"Actually," Mrs. Crockett said, "she's a friend of mine, and a very demure young lady except when she's modeling. But recently she's been thinking some of making modeling a career. There was a change in her status, and—"

Sylvia Hadley laughed and said, "Oh, don't pull any punches, Phyllis."

She turned to me. "My husband turned out to be a perfect heel. He went through everything I had, then picked up with another woman and left me high and dry. Phyllis is awfully nice trying to pretend this is a neighborly favor I'm doing for her, but actually she's paying me for it.

"I knew she painted and hired models, and I felt that I had

what it took, so I asked her to pay me the same rate she paid the models.

"Now there you have it, Mr. Lam, and there's no need for any embarrassment or covering up. After all, I'm working for a living....We do have a break every once in a while, and there you have the story in a nutshell."

I looked around at some of the paintings and said, "Evidently you have rather steady work."

Phyllis laughed. "I don't know whether you noticed, Mr. Lam, but she has an absolutely divine figure. I want to put it on canvas in as many different poses as I can."

"I noticed," I said dryly.

"The paintings?"

"The figure."

"I thought you had," Sylvia remarked demurely.

"Your husband's not available?" I asked Mrs. Crockett.

"My husband," she said, "has what is known as a hibernating suite. It's most annoying. He goes in there every so often when he has a job to do and closes and locks the door. And when he's in there, nothing, absolutely *nothing*, disturbs him, Mr. Lam. He isn't available to his wife, to his friends, or to anyone.

"That's where he writes some of his travel books. He sits in there and dictates by the hour...."

"A secretary?" I asked.

"No secretary. A dictating machine. He has a little kitchenette in which he keeps provisions—the sort of food which can be pre-pared without too much trouble; eggs, canned beans, chili con carne, Spanish rice, brown bread....That's one thing about Dean. He's a pretty good cook and he can get by on a diet of concentrated proteins without any fresh green stuff...sometimes he'll stay in there two or three days at a time."

"So I take it he's not interested in the recovery of his blowgun."

"Of course he's interested, terribly interested. But he wouldn't want to know anything about it until after he comes out of hibernation."

"Could you tell me when that would be?"

She shrugged good-looking shoulders.

I stood the blowgun in a corner. "That will be all right here?"

"Yes. However in the world did you recover it, Mr. Lam, and how did you recover it so soon?"

I said, "It's rather a long story, but rather a simple story."

Sylvia Hadley looked from one to the other of us. "The blowgun was stolen?" she asked.

Phyllis nodded.

"Anything else missing?" Sylvia asked. And I had the feeling there was more than casual interest in her voice.

"A jade Buddha," Mrs. Crockett said. "The mate to the jade Buddha that disappeared three weeks ago."

"You mean that beautiful piece of smooth, green jade carved into a Buddha contemplating nirvana, with that expression of rapt, serene concentration?"

"That's the one," Phyllis said. "Dean made quite a scene about it."

"Oh, but he should. Good heavens, that's…why, that's one of the most beautiful pieces of carving I've ever seen. I'd…oh, I'd *love* to have even a second-rate duplicate of that. I was going to ask Dean if it wouldn't be possible to cast that in plaster of Paris and— You mean it's *gone*?"

"It's gone," Phyllis said.

"Oh, for Heaven's sake," Sylvia Hadley said.

I glanced across at Mrs. Crockett. "Don't you think your husband would be sufficiently interested in the return of the blowgun to make it advisable to interrupt him?"

"You *can't* interrupt him."

"Surely there's a door," I said. "You can knock on the door."

"There are two doors. Both are locked. There's a closet in between them. I don't think you could hear a knock."

"There's no telephone where he is?"

She shook her head. "It's a part of the house that he had specially designed. I tell you, it's absolutely out of the question except for a major emergency unless—"

"Unless what?"

"Unless he isn't working and I can attract his attention through the window."

I waited.

She bit her lip thoughtfully, picked up the blowgun and said, "Come with me, please."

She left Sylvia Hadley sitting there in the thin robe, legs crossed, the robe knotted at the waist, feeding into a knot and falling away from the knot in two revealing Vs.

I followed her into a hallway. She opened a bathroom door, laughed a bit and said, "Crowd over close to the window and we'll see."

I moved over to the narrow bathroom window. She opened the frosted glass and leaned over so close to me that I could feel her cheek brushing mine as she pointed at a lighted window perhaps twenty-five feet across an air well and some fifteen feet higher than our level.

"That's his place up there," she said. "Sometimes he has the drapes closed and— No, this time he hasn't got the drapes closed....Sometimes he's dictating to a dictating machine, and then he sits in one place. Sometimes he's thinking and then he walks the floor. If he walks the floor back and forth past the window, we can signal him with a flashlight."

"Just a minute," she said, and stepped from the bathroom.

She was back in seconds with a five-cell flashlight.

"If we see him walking, I'll signal him," she said. "But I'm not going to be responsible for the consequences. We may get a terrific tongue-lashing. He doesn't like to be disturbed when he's up there."

"I take it your husband is a man of highly individual tastes," I said.

"You can say that again."

She pushed close to me, then said, "Look, this is an awkward position. I'm crowded in between the john and the wall…. Here."

She shifted her position with a lithe wriggle of her body, put her left arm around my neck and up close to me. "There," she said, "that's better—I was being crowded."

"If your husband happens to look out and see us now," I said, "he'll perhaps give us two tongue-lashings. We must look rather intimate from up there."

"Don't be silly," she said. "How can two people make love in a bathroom with their heads sticking out of a bathroom window?"

"You'll admit we're rather close."

"Of course we're close. Good heavens, what is that, a fountain pen in your inside pocket?"

"A pencil."

"Well, for Heaven's sake, take it out and switch it to the other side."

I took the pencil out and dropped it into the side pocket of my coat.

"I don't believe he's walking around…." She lowered her voice. "Didn't you say something about that jade Buddha?"

"I said I was about to recover the jade Buddha."

"Oh, I thought you said you'd recovered it."

"I guess I wasn't speaking very plainly."

"Oh, don't bother to apologize. It's my ears. Sometimes I hear and sometimes I don't….Well, Mr. Lam, this has been a very enjoyable experience in one way, but from the standpoint of husband communicating, I guess it's— Oh, well. I'm going to take a chance."

She put on the flashlight and directed it against the plate-glass window.

"There's an open window to the right of that," I said. "Where does that lead?"

"That leads into the little closet I was telling you about. There are two doors in the closet. One into his place and one into the main house. The closet separates the two doors. He keeps them both closed and both locked."

"Let's try that open window."

The beam of the spotlight was powerful enough to go through the open window, penetrate the late afternoon light and illuminate a section of the wall showing a shelf littered with half a dozen objects which couldn't readily be identified.

Abruptly she switched off the light. "I'm frightened," she said. "Come on, let's pass it up. I'll tell him as soon as he comes out of hibernation. He'll be very, very thrilled, Mr. Lam, that you have recovered that blowgun. Could you tell me how you did it?"

"Not now," I said.

"Why?" she pouted.

"It might interfere with getting back the jade idol."

She lowered the window, which placed a pane of frosted glass between us and the penthouse apartment across the air well. I tried to move out of the corner. She twisted and stood facing me very close, her body pushed up against me.

"You know something, Donald?" she asked in a low voice.

"What?"

"You're nice," she said. And then suddenly she had her arm around my neck, pulling my head down to the hot circle of her lips. The fingers of her other hand came up and stroked my cheek, then slid around to the back of my neck and tickled the short hairs just above the neckline.

After a moment she broke away. "Oh, you're wonderful!" she sighed. And then, instantly practical, said, "Here. Here's some cleaning tissue. Wipe off the lipstick. I don't want Sylvia to know I…I…became impulsive."

She laughed, whirled toward the bathroom mirror, took out a lipstick and deftly started making up her mouth with the aid of the lipstick and her little finger.

"All right?" she asked.

I surveyed my image in the mirror. "I guess so. A little short of breath, but all right."

She opened the bathroom door and walked casually out to the studio, saying, "No go, Sylvia. We couldn't raise him."

She turned to me, cool and languid, and said with a casual manner of dismissal, "Well, I guess there's no use, Mr. Lam, I'll let him know that you've recovered the blowgun."

"And are on the trail of the idol," Sylvia Hadley said.

"And are on the trail of the idol," Phyllis Crockett echoed.

I hesitated a moment.

"Well," Phyllis said brightly, "I guess the recess is over, Sylvia. Let's get to work."

Without a word, Sylvia arose lightly from the chair, untied the cord, tossed the robe over the back of the chair, walked up to the modeling platform and resumed her nude pose with the manner of a professional.

Phyllis Crockett picked up her smock, put it back on, ran her thumb through the hole in the palette, selected a brush and said over her shoulder, "Awfully nice of you to come, Mr. Lam."

"Don't mention it," I told her.

She put the brush to the paint, then started making brush marks on the canvas.

"Thanks a lot," I said.

"Okay," she called, her eyes still on the canvas. "Don't mention it."

"Glad I met you, Miss Hadley," I called. And then couldn't resist adding as I put my hand on the knob of the door, "Hope I get to see more of you."

She smiled at that one, and I gently closed the door.

Chapter Ten

At nine-thirty in the morning I rang up Crockett's place. The well-modulated tones of Melvin Otis Olney came over the phone. "Who is this talking, please?"

"Donald Lam, Olney."

"Oh, yes, Mr. Lam."

"I recovered the missing blowgun."

"You what!" he shouted into the telephone.

"Recovered the missing blowgun. Didn't Mrs. Crockett tell you?"

"I haven't seen Mrs. Crockett."

"Well, I recovered it and left it with her."

His tone was coldly formal. "I am afraid you shouldn't have done that. The property should have been returned to Dean Crockett."

I didn't like the dignified manner in which he tried to rebuke me.

"Crockett was closeted in his hibernating room. He wouldn't come out. He has no telephone in there; no one else was home, and so I left it with Mrs. Crockett. What's wrong with that? It's community property, isn't it?"

"I— Yes, I suppose so."

"Okay, I left it with her. Now I have the jade Buddha. What do I do with that?"

"You have what?"

"I have the jade Buddha," I told him. "What's the matter with your connection? Can't you hear?"

"My ears hear," Olney said, "but it's hard for me to believe what they hear. I— Well, Lam, this is incredible."

"What's incredible about it?"

"Recovering both articles like that."

"That's what we were hired for, isn't it?"

"Yes, I know, but…and in such a short time. It's absolutely, utterly incredible. Mr. Crockett simply won't believe his ears when I tell him."

"Well, perhaps he'll believe his eyes when he sees the jade statue. Now, what do I do about delivering this jade Buddha?"

"You come right up with it."

"Wait a minute," I said. "I'd better talk with Mr. Crockett himself. You didn't like the idea of me leaving the blowgun with Mrs. Crockett, and, unless Crockett is there—"

"He's here."

"In circulation?"

"He will be. He told me to be here at nine o'clock, prepared to discuss a matter with him, and he wanted his secretary here, prepared to transcribe some records that he has been dictating."

"He's there?"

"I tell you, he will be by the time you get here. Come on up."

"Mrs. Crockett didn't tell you about the blowgun?"

"Not me. This is the first I'd heard."

"You might ask her where it is," I said.

"I think we'll let Mr. Crockett handle that end of it, Mr. Lam. When will you be up here?"

"In about twenty minutes."

"Very well. We'll be expecting you."

I got in the battered-up agency heap and drove up to the apartment house.

This time it wasn't necessary for me to be announced. They treated me at the front desk as though I had been an honored

guest with an engraved invitation and their job was to roll out
the red carpet.

"Good morning, Mr. Lam," the clerk said, all smiles. "You're
going up to the Crockett penthouse. They're expecting you.
You know the way. Just take the elevator to the twentieth floor.
They'll meet you with the elevator to the penthouse."

"Thanks," I said.

I went on up to the twentieth floor, walked down to the door
marked 20-S, which, from the outside, looked exactly like the
door to any other apartment. The door was unlocked. I opened
this door and found myself in the anteroom. The concealed
slide was open to show the telephone and a printed sign over
the telephone saying, "Press button and pick up receiver."

I pressed the button, picked up the receiver, and a man's
voice said, "Yes, who is it, please?"

"Mr. Lam— Who is this? It isn't Olney."

"No, sir, this is Wilbur C. Denton, Mr. Crockett's secretary. I
am sending the elevator down for you, Mr. Lam."

"Very well," I said.

I hung up the telephone and waited.

A minute or so later the elevator came down and I went on up.

I wondered if I was being X-rayed. I presumed I was.

I stepped out of the elevator, and a tall, droopy individual
extended a limp hand. "I'm Mr. Denton, Mr. Crockett's secretary, Mr. Lam. I'm glad to meet you."

I let go of the hand as soon as I could, and said, "Where's
Olney?"

"Mr. Olney is on the telephone."

"All right. Where's Crockett?"

"Mr. Crockett will be here momentarily."

"What do I do? Sit down and wait?"

"It will only be a moment, I'm certain....Mr. Crockett is

getting out a very important matter this morning and asked me to be here in readiness. However, I know that Mr. Olney feels the nature of your business is so important, Mr. Crockett wouldn't want anything to interfere with seeing you."

Denton smiled a watered-down version of Olney's cordial manner and led the way into a part of the house I hadn't been in before. It was a room fixed up as a transcribing office, with an electric typewriter, a transcribing machine, some filing cases and four or five fairly comfortable chairs.

"Just have a seat," he said. "I'll go right on with my work, if you don't mind."

"I don't mind."

Denton fitted earplugs into his ears, held his long, bony fingers poised over the keyboard of the typewriter for a moment, and then came down on the keyboard like a piano player putting on a speed exhibition.

I sat there and watched him, absolutely fascinated. The staccato of the keys was broken only by the tinkle of the bell as the carriage reached the end of its run. The way the guy was typing it seemed that the carriage went from right to left just about as fast as the electric return whipped it back from left to right.

No time at all and the guy had reached the end of the paper and was feeding another sheet into the typewriter.

The door opened, and Melvin Otis Olney came in, all smiles and diffusive cordiality.

"Well, well, Lam," he exclaimed. "The demon detective—you've certainly hung up a record for efficiency, speed of operation and satisfactory services. How are you?"

He grabbed my right and pumped it up and down. His left hand was patting my back.

Denton never looked up from his work, his eyes watching the typing, his fingers banging the keyboard.

"You've met Denton?" Olney asked.

"I've met him."

"Well, come on in. Mr. Crockett wants to see you."

He led me through the office into a private office and tapped gently on a door at the back of the private office. It looked like a closet door.

There was no answer and he knocked again.

When there was still no answer, he pressed a bell button, an ingeniously concealed button somewhere in the wall. Even watching him, I couldn't see where the button was. It was a cunningly contrived bit of inlay that could probably have been found with a magnifying glass, but if a person didn't know where it was, he certainly couldn't put his thumb on it. I only knew it was there because I heard the sound of muted chimes as he pushed his thumb.

Olney looked at his wrist watch and said under his breath, "That's strange."

I said nothing.

A woman's voice said, "What seems to be the trouble, Melvin?"

I turned and saw Mrs. Crockett, attired in a filmy negligee, standing in back of us. The light was coming through the doorway behind her and her figure was silhouetted with disconcerting frankness. She didn't seem to give it a thought.

Olney's voice was coldly formal. "Nothing is the trouble, Mrs. Crockett."

She saw me then and said, "Oh, good morning, Mr. Lam.... Oh, I guess I'm a little visible here in the doorway, am I not?"

She laughed and pulled the negligee a little more tightly around her, which didn't change the visibility too much.

"Where's Dean?" she asked.

"In his private study," Olney said. "He told me that he would be ready for work at nine o'clock this morning and wanted me to be sure that Wilbur was here. He said he had some important documents to get out."

"When did he tell you?"

"Yesterday afternoon."

"I thought he was locked up in his study all day."

"He was out for about half an hour. I think you were in your studio."

Olney pressed the button again, and again the chimes sounded.

"There's an emergency key somewhere," Olney said. "I think we'd better look in. There's just a chance that—"

"No, no, no," Mrs. Crockett exclaimed. "He'd never forgive anyone for that. When he's in there, his privacy must be held absolutely inviolate."

"But suppose he's sick?"

"He...he couldn't get so sick he couldn't get out here."

"I don't know," Olney said. "People can get sick so suddenly they can't even get out of a chair....Where's that emergency key?"

"It....it's in the safe. But I wouldn't touch it for the world. I wouldn't think of it. That would—"

"Where in the safe?"

"In the upper right-hand drawer."

"You have the combination?"

"Yes."

"I think we'd better open the safe and use that key."

She shook her head.

Olney said with cold formality. "Very well, Mrs. Crockett, the decision is yours and, therefore, the responsibility will be yours." He looked at his watch and said, "It is seven minutes past ten, Mr. Lam. Will you please remember that I wanted to use the emergency key and go in at this time, and that Mrs. Crockett refused—"

"Wait a minute," she interrupted. "Where do you get that noise? You're not going to throw anything like that off on my shoulders."

"Then get us the key."

She hesitated a moment, then said, "Very well. Mr. Lam, will you please note that it is now seven minutes and thirty seconds past ten o'clock and that Mr. Olney has advised me that unless I get the emergency key and open this door, he will hold me personally responsible."

I stood there without saying anything.

Olney said to me, "That's quite all right, Mr. Lam. Whenever *I* do anything, *I'm* willing to take the responsibility."

"Just a minute," Phyllis Crockett said sweetly, "I'll get you the key."

She walked through the doorway and disappeared.

"There has to be something wrong," Olney said in an undertone. "He likes to go in there where he can get away from her and not be interrupted. His wife is inclined to take his literary labors lightly and bothers him at the most inopportune times with the most inane comments, such as what he wanted for dinner or whether he wanted to talk with someone on the telephone. The worst of it is, she has no discretion.…However, I shouldn't be discussing the matter with you. I trust you'll consider my remarks personal, confidential and caused by the fact I'm just a little worried. I don't know what's happening, but I can tell you this. Dean Crockett is in trouble of some sort. I'm afraid he's had a heart attack or a stroke. That bell button is a secret signal that only his wife and I know about—see if you can find it."

He stood to one side and I looked over the wooden panel, then I looked it over again. I couldn't see a thing.

"Now watch my thumb," Olney said.

He stood up in front of the panel, ran his fingers over the panel for a moment, then suddenly jabbed with his thumb.

I heard the chimes again sounding in the interior.

"Okay," I said, "I got it that time."

Olney looked at me with a patronizing smile. "See if you can find it," he said.

I stepped up to the panel and ran my fingers over the wood just as he had done. As I did so, I moved the toe of my left foot so it was up against the baseboard in exactly the position his foot had been.

I pretended to jab with my thumb, but at the same time exerted pressure with the toe of my boot.

The chimes sounded.

I stepped back.

Olney looked at me with a most peculiar expression on his face. "By God," he said, "you *are* smart!"

I didn't say anything.

The door opened and Mrs. Crockett came in with the key. She said, "I'm letting you take this key, Olney, because you have assured me that—"

Olney didn't wait for her to finish. He snatched at the key, fitted it in the lock in the door and shot back the bolt.

All three of us started through the doorway, then all three of us stopped. The door opened to the closet that I had seen the day before from Mrs. Crockett's studio.

Dean Crockett the Second was sprawled out on the floor on his back, his knees doubled, the feet back under him. There was a dart from a blowgun embedded in his chest a short distance below the throat. The guy had undoubtedly been dead for some time.

From where I stood, I gave the place a quick once-over. There were shelves pretty well loaded with curios, canned foods, stationery, notebooks and odds and ends.

At the upper back of the little closet near the ceiling was another dart that had been shot with sufficient force so that the point was deeply embedded in the wood.

"Good God!" Olney exclaimed.

"Look, look," Phyllis Crockett screamed. "In his throat. A dart from the blowgun."

"And another one sticking in that shelf up there," I said, pointing.

Mrs. Crockett leaned forward and reached up to grasp the dart in the shelf.

"Leave that alone!" I said.

She turned sharply at the sound of my voice. "Why... Mr. Lam, you startled me. What do you mean, leave it alone? And who are you to speak to me in that tone of authority?"

I said, "Get away from there. That dart is evidence. You touch anything in there and you'll be very, very sorry."

"What do you mean, I'll be sorry?" she asked.

I said, "The angle of the dart in the wood shows trajectory. You can see that the path of trajectory runs through the open window, and I would say offhand just about down to the bathroom window in your studio."

She looked at me in openmouthed amazement.

"You go in and pull that dart out," I said, "and they'll claim that your first consideration was not for your husband but to hurry in and try to obliterate evidence that indicated the blowgun had been fired by you through your bathroom window in a desire to become a fascinating widow. Now, get out of here and leave things just as they are. I'm going to notify the police."

Olney turned to me coldly and said, "It seems to me that I am forced to agree with Mrs. Crockett. You're taking on a lot of authority."

"You're damn right I am," I told him, "I'm a licensed private detective. I know the procedure in these matters. Both of you get out of here and close that door. I'm telephoning the Homicide Squad."

"And if we don't choose to obey you?" Olney asked.

I said, "Then, when I tell the police that you loused up the evidence, they'll know it was deliberate."

He grinned at me and said, "That, of course, does it. It's the approach you used with Mrs. Crockett, and I must say it's effective. Come on, Mrs. Crockett, we'll step out of here and close the room. And I think, in order to pull the fangs of this little rattlesnake who has suddenly started to hiss and sound his rattles, we'll let him hold the key until the police get here. In that way, we can't be accused of removing any evidence."

He was pushing Phyllis Crockett back and pulling the door closed all the time he was talking. As we stepped out, he twisted the key in the lock.

I reached out and took the key and said, "That's one of the best talks you ever made. Even if you aren't smart enough to realize it...or are you?"

Chapter Eleven

Bertha Cool's friend, Frank Sellers, was in charge of the detail from Homicide Squad that came up to the apartment.

Frank Sellers had a certain grudging respect for Bertha Cool's hard-boiled outlook on life. He'd never been entirely certain about me. When I came into the firm, Sellers had made no secret of his disapproval. Bertha pointed out in vain that she needed someone younger, quick-thinking and fast on his feet. Sellers simply couldn't see a small guy. He worshiped brawn. I remember hearing him say to her one time, "Where the hell do brains get you in this world, Bertha? It takes impact to get you anywhere."

Sellers said, "Well, well, it's none other than our pint-sized friend, Donald Lam, the brainy fugitive from a law school. Now, what the hell are you doing here?"

"At the moment," I said, "I've finished calling police to report a murder, and I'm headed out for the office as soon as I've answered the necessary questions—unless, of course, you want to spend the time in personal badinage."

"What the hell's badinage?" Sellers asked with instant suspicion.

"A synthetic substitute for insinuations of guilty participation translated to a plane of pseudofacetiousness."

"You sonofabitch," Sellers said angrily. "Where's Crockett?"

"Here's the key. He's behind that door. You'll find some interesting clues."

"After you got through messing with them," Sellers said. He took the key and opened the door.

He stood for a long time in the doorway, then he motioned to two of the other men to come and join him.

They stood there silently.

Sellers pointed to the feathered dart that was stuck in the wood, then pointed to the open window, then down to the studio apartment on the other side of the light well. "Find out who has that apartment down there," he said to one of the men. "Then get the manager of the place and we'll get a passkey and take a look."

"There's no need for that," Mrs. Crockett said. "*I* happen to be the one who occupies that apartment."

"What's the idea of living up here and having an apartment down there?"

"That's my studio. It's where I work."

"What do *you* work at?" he asked suspiciously.

"She paints," I told him.

"How long you been connected with this thing?" Sellers asked me.

"Since three days ago."

"How come?"

"They gave a party. Crockett had suffered losses at previous gatherings, so he retained Bertha to see that—"

"So he did, so he did," Sellers interrupted, grinning. "I remember reading about it in the paper. And how did Bertha get along with the guests?"

"Wonderful."

"How is the old gal?"

"Running true to form."

"Some babe," he said enthusiastically. Then he added, by way of explanation to one of his men, "There's a gal who would just as soon gouge your eye out as break your arm....Okay, Lam, you take these two people back into one of the other rooms. I'm going to leave it to you to see they don't touch any-thing that might be evidence. We're going in with the body and look around....How does it happen the crime is just being discovered? He's evidently been dead for quite a while."

"I just came up here a few minutes ago," I said, "but I under-stand he has this as a secret den. He shut himself in there when he wanted to be absolutely undisturbed. It's a rule of the house that no one disturbs him for *anything* when he's in here."

"How about meals?"

"You can see the canned goods on the shelf, and I under-stand there's a kitchenette adjoining the place."

"How far in did you go?"

"Just as far as the doorway."

"How about the others?"

"No farther. I turned everyone back."

"Okay," he said. "Go in there and sit down. I'll be out and talk with you after we've looked things over a bit. There'll be a police photographer up here any minute, a fingerprint man, and a deputy coroner. Tell them where we are....Any way of getting up here except by going through all that rigmarole at the elevator?"

"That's it," I said, "at least as far as I know, unless you can get up on some other section of the roof and walk across."

"Okay, okay. Go on and keep these people occupied. I'll look around."

We all went into the living room and sat down.

"How about a drink?" Phyllis Crockett asked as casually as though it had been an ordinary social gathering.

"I think, under the circumstances, it might be better to wait a little while," I said. "Sellers can get a little rough on occasion, and since *he* can't drink while he's on duty, he might resent smelling liquor on our breaths....I gave you a blowgun yesterday evening, Mrs. Crockett. Where is it?"

"Why, right where you left it down in my studio," she said. "Do you think they'll want it?"

"They'll want it."

"All right," she said, in a casual manner, "I'll go get it."

"You'll stay right here," I said. "Don't go down to that studio until you go with Sellers."

"Why not? It's my studio."

"True, it is. However, being suspicious is Seller's job. He'll claim you were dashing down there to conceal evidence or get rid of something incriminating."

"What do you mean, incriminating?"

"*I* don't mean anything," I said. "Sellers will be the one to explain that to you."

We were silent for a few seconds. The rattle of the type-writer from the office was nerve-racking.

I said to Olney, "It might be a good idea to tell Denton that the man he was working for isn't going to sign any more pay-checks."

Olney said, "You tell him."

I thought I saw a glance flash between him and Phyllis Crockett, so I simply sat down, lit a cigarette and said, "After all, I guess it isn't important. He'll find it out soon, and probably Sellers will want all those records transcribed anyway."

"Well, *I'm* going to have some coffee," Phyllis Crockett said. "*My* stomach has butterflies."

"I'll join you with some coffee," Olney said. "Let me make it."

"No, no. I'll make it."

Olney smiled at me. "If you'll excuse us, Lam," he said, "I'll help Mrs. Crockett with the coffee. We'll be back in a minute."

I got up out of the chair and said, "If you'll both excuse me. I'll help both of you with the coffee."

I walked out in the kitchen with them.

Phyllis Crockett got out an electric coffee-making outfit. "We don't do cooking here," she explained, "just coffee, and occasionally we boil eggs and fry bacon. But for the most part we have food sent in or we eat out, or if we're entertaining, we have a caterer handle the job."

"How's the cream?" Olney asked.

"I don't use it," Mrs. Crockett said.

"I can't enjoy coffee without cream and sugar," Olney told her.

She opened the icebox. He took out a square paste-board cream container, went to the drawer containing the spoons, took out a spoon, poured a little cream in the spoon, tasted it, then made a face and said, "Sour."

"That's a shame," Mrs. Crockett said.

"It's all right," he told her. "I can dash down and have some more cream by the time the coffee is ready, or...perhaps under the circumstances I shouldn't leave. They may want something....Lam, would you mind terribly just dropping down in the elevator. There's a delicatessen store just two doors down the street, and—"

"I'd mind terribly," I interrupted. "So would Sellers."

I took a spoon from the drawer, tasted the cream and said, "And besides this cream is completely sweet."

"It tasted sour to me."

"Something wrong with your taste."

"That's what comes of having fruit juice," Phyllis Crockett said brightly. "I know that when I've had grapefruit juice and then try to taste cream, it *always* tastes sour. How about you, Mr. Lam? Shall we put your name in the coffeepot?"

"You don't need to put my name in," I said, "but you might put Frank Sellers' name in. He's quite a coffee drinker."

"I see no reason on our part to wine and dine the police," Olney said.

"Don't wine 'em and don't dine 'em," I said, "but if you coffee them, you sometimes get them in a more amiable mood. Sellers likes coffee, and if his nose gets the aroma of the coffee but he isn't offered any, he might not be so cooperative."

Olney tried to save face by saying, "We don't give a damn whether he's cooperative or not." But after he had said it, he looked significantly at Phyllis Crockett and said, "It might be a good idea to put on the large coffee urn, Mrs. Crockett." She opened a drawer, took out a big silver urn and said, "This holds a gallon of coffee. How much shall I make, Mr. Lam?"

"That's up to you," I said.

"Dump in lots of coffee and fill it up," Olney said. "After all, Lam has a point there. Cops like coffee."

Phyllis Crockett dumped in coffee, poured in water, turned on the electricity. She went to the refrigerator, took out some frozen orange juice, diluted it with water, stirred it with a spoon and raised her eyebrows in silent interrogation.

I shook my head. Olney nodded his.

She filled two glasses and they silently drank the orange juice.

The door opened and Frank Sellers came in. "All right, Lam," he said, "give me the low-down."

I said, "This is Mrs. Crockett, the widow."

I saw her eyes widen as I said widow, but instantly she was in control of her features once more.

"Yeah, I've talked with her already," Sellers said. "Now, who's the other one?"

"That's Melvin Otis Olney," I said, "the general manager, director of publicity, and, I believe, he was Mr. Crockett's right hand. The guy who's pounding the typewriter in the other room is named Wilbur Denton. He's a secretary. I don't think he knows of Crockett's murder. He doesn't live here. I'm not certain whether Olney does or doesn't."

"You live here?" Sellers asked Olney.

It was Mrs. Crockett who answered the question. "Certainly not."

"Okay," Sellers said, "let's have it. I want it condensed in a nutshell....That coffee in that electric gadget?"

She nodded.

"Good, I'll have a cup when it's ready. Now, I'll take you first, Mrs. Crockett. How long have you been married?"

"Three years."

"Been married before?"

"Once."

"Widowed or divorced?"

"Divorced."

"How about your present husband?"

"He'd been married twice before."

"When did you see him last?"

"It's been...well, I didn't see him all day yesterday. By the time I got up he had retired to his study, and—"

"What do you mean, retired to his study?"

"Just what I said. When he goes in there he closes both doors. Usually the door into the main part of the house is closed, and the door from the closet into his study is closed."

"What does he go in there for?"

"To work."

"I notice he has a dictating machine in there."

"That's right."

"But I can't find where he dictated anything yesterday."

"He must have. He was in there all day....Of course, sometimes he is thinking up the proper approach."

"He does a lot of dictating?"

"Travel articles. He loves to travel. His whole life is devoted to that."

"And you paint?"

"Yes."

"How long have you had that studio down there on the other floor?"

"About six months, I guess."

"I'm going to want to go down there and look around. Any objection?"

"No, I'll take you down there."

"Just give me a key," Sellers said, "and I'll look around by myself."

"I'd rather be with you."

"Okay, if you want. We'll go down after a while."

He turned to Olney. "What do you know about all this?"

"I work rather closely with Mr. Crockett," Olney said. "I know that he went into his study yesterday, but he came out at about…oh, I don't know, perhaps four-thirty or five o'clock. He gave me some records which were to be transcribed and asked me to have the secretary, Mr. Denton, be here at nine o'clock in the morning. He also told me he wanted to discuss some matters with me at nine o'clock, so to be sure and be here. Then he did some telephoning and went back to his private study, closing the doors."

"Know who he telephoned to?"

"No."

"His secretary came in this morning?"

"That's right. He's pounding away on the records."

"Sounds like a pretty good worker," Sellers said, cocking an ear to the sound of the typewriter.

"He's very rapid and exceedingly accurate."

"Wish I had him to type out my reports," Sellers said. "My two-finger technique isn't quite that good. I have what they call a heavy touch."

"You would," I told him.

"That'll do from you, Pint Size," he said. "What the hell are you doing here?"

"I came up to discuss a matter with Mr. Crockett."

"What matter?"

"The matter on which I was employed."

"A jade Buddha had been stolen," Olney said. "Mr. Lam told me over the telephone that he had recovered it."

Sellers raised his eyebrows. I nodded.

"Where is it?" Sellers asked.

"Where I can get it when it's needed."

"Where did you find it? Who had it?"

"That may or may not be significant," I said. And then, as I caught his eye, I slowly winked.

"Okay, Pint Size, okay," Sellers said. "We'll get to the Buddha later."

"The blowgun was also stolen," Olney said.

Sellers jerked to stiff attention as though the chair had been wired. "Blowgun, eh?"

"That's right."

"That's what killed him, wasn't it?"

"It would seem that way."

"All right, what about the blowgun?"

"Mr. Lam recovered that, I believe, yesterday."

Sellers looked at me. "The hell," he said.

"And," Olney went on, "I believe he said he gave it to Mrs. Crockett."

"Well, what do you know?" Sellers observed, looking at me and then shifting his eyes to Phyllis Crockett. "You got it?"

"It's in my studio."

"You mean this place down there?" Sellers asked, pointing his finger.

She nodded.

"What's it doing down there?"

"Mr. Lam came yesterday to see my…my husband. There was no one here at the time, and so I had left word at the desk that if anyone called I was to be notified in my studio. The phone rang there, and Mr. Lam said that he had the blowgun—or I believe he asked to come up. He wanted to see Mr. Crockett, and I guess it was then that he told me about the blowgun. I don't remember the sequence of events very clearly."

"What do you know!" Sellers said, his manner showing his keen interest. "And did he have the blowgun with him?"

"Yes."

"And what did he do with it?"

"He gave it to me."

Sellers scratched his head. "Now, Mrs. Crockett, I'm going to ask you something. I don't want you to get mad about it. I don't mean to imply anything. I'm just asking questions. Down in that studio apartment of yours there's a window, a little oblong window that looks as though it might be the window of a bathroom. That window is almost directly opposite that open window in the closet there in your husband's private study."

"That's right."

"Now then," Sellers went on, "I want you to think carefully. I want you to answer this question, and I don't want you to change your answer later on. I want the truth and I want it now. Did you or did you not, at any time after you received that blowgun, open that bathroom window?"

"Why, certainly," she said.

"Oh, you did?"

"Why, of course. Mr. Lam and I opened it together."

"Well, well, well," Sellers said, looking at me. "And what were you doing opening it together?"

"She was trying to get her husband's attention," I said. "She had a flashlight, and—"

"Never mind. Pint Size," Sellers said to me. "I'm doing this. Why did you open the window, Mrs. Crockett?"

"I wanted to attract my husband's attention. I wanted him to come to the window."

"And how did you plan on doing that?"

"By using a flashlight."

"Was it daytime or nighttime?"

"It was daytime, but it was…late in the afternoon."

"A flashlight *wouldn't* shine across there."

"This was a big flashlight," I said. "A big five-cell flashlight."

"Now, you keep out of this, Pint Size," Sellers said to me. "I'm—huh— *What* did you say?"

"A five-cell flashlight," I said.

"Well, what do you know!" Sellers said. "What were you doing with a five-cell flashlight down there, Mrs. Crockett?"

"I have it there," she said, "because sometimes, when I want to attract my husband's attention, I can do it by shining a powerful flashlight either in the window of that closet or on the window of his study. If it happens he's in there and wants to come to the window, he'll come and open it and I can call a message across to him."

"So you keep that flashlight down there for the sole purpose of signaling your husband?"

"Yes."

One of the other officers entered the room. "Inspector Giddings," Sellers said. It was an explanation, not an introduction.

"How about giving me the keys and letting me go down there and look around?" Sellers asked Mrs. Crockett.

"I think it would be better if Mrs. Crockett went down there with you," I said.

Sellers looked at me with uncordial eyes. "Well, now, where did *you* get any call to put in *your* two bits' worth, Pint Size? We're investigating a murder and I'm just pigheaded enough to think I'm going to investigate it my own way."

I looked at him and said, "Then suppose you find something else down there and put a nice little label on it and bring it into court as evidence, and some smart lawyer gets you on the witness stand on cross-examination and says, 'How do we know you didn't plant that stuff down there?'"

"Now *you're* telling me how to do *my* job," Sellers said.

"That's right."

Sellers thought it over for a moment, said, "You could make yourself awfully unpopular shooting off your face, but I'm going to let it pass for the moment. I'll take Inspector Giddings along with me if you're sure that meets with your approval. And since you've pointed out that some smart lawyer is apt to criticize the way I'm going at things here, I think I'll take all you folks into the office and we'll tell this secretary about his boss. And then we'll leave you with a chaperone to see that you don't get wandering around anywhere.

"I take it your master-mind won't find any loopholes there, Mr. Lam.

"Now, Mrs. Crockett, if you wouldn't mind giving me the key to your studio…"

"You don't have to, you know," I said to her. "If he wants to search the place you have a right to—"

Inspector Giddings moved fast for a man of his size. He grabbed me by the back of the neck, putting his middle finger and thumb in at points where they pressed the nerves just under my ears, an old police trick for handling persons who proved difficult in picture shows or behind the steering wheels of automobiles.

"Just about one more crack out of you," he said, "and I'm going to teach you something."

I had to squirm with the pain, but I said, "You get your hands off me, or *I'll* teach *you* something."

Inspector Giddings shook me until I was seeing double. Sellers, watching him, said casually, "I think you're out of line, Inspector."

Giddings paused to look at Sellers in surprise. "You mean you're going to stand for that kind of talk? You're going to let him pull that stuff and get away with it?"

"Don't make any mistake about the guy," Sellers cautioned. "He has brains. Now, just to keep the record straight, Lam, are you employed by Mrs. Crockett?"

I was having trouble getting my centers of speech to work. "He is employed by me," Mrs. Crockett said.

"To do what?" Sellers asked.

"To try and find out who is responsible for my husband's death."

Sellers' eyes narrowed. "That takes in lots of territory."

"Very well," she said, "it takes in lots of territory. I want to cooperate with the officers, but I want to find out who killed my husband."

"That's what *we're* paid for," Sellers said.

"I understand that, and so does Mr. Lam. I'm quite certain you'll continue to draw exactly the same compensation and work with the same efficiency. Now then, if you want my key to the studio, here it is."

She handed the key to Sellers, who nodded to Inspector

Giddings. "All right, Thad," he said, "let's go break the news to Denton, then go on down and take a look at this place. You understand, Mrs. Crockett, that you're perfectly free to come along if you wish to do so."

"It's quite all right," she said, "I have nothing to conceal. I have the utmost confidence in your integrity and ability. Although," she said, glaring at Inspector Giddings, "I don't like *your* brutality!"

Giddings said, "Well, there's nothing in the law that says some private eye has the right to keep busting in when the police are trying to investigate a murder."

"On the contrary," she said. "I think Mr. Lam was entirely within his rights. He was being courteous, respectful and co-operative. And your unprovoked attack was, in my opinion, the act of a bully. It is my own first experience with police brutality and I don't like it."

Giddings stood looking at her, his face dark red with anger.

Frank Sellers sighed. "Come on, Thad," he said, "we're not getting anywhere here. Let's go down and look at that studio."

Chapter Twelve

A third officer herded us into the office where Wilbur Denton was banging away at the typewriter.

The officer tapped Denton on the shoulder, said, "The whistle's blown."

Denton looked up in surprise, said, "What do you mean?" The officer took a leather folder from his pocket, showed him the badge and his I.D. card. "We're taking charge." Denton looked up at the officer, then looked around at us. His face was a mask of startled surprise.

"Dean Crockett has been murdered," I explained.

The officer turned to me. "I'm doing the talking here."

"Go ahead and do it then. What's the use of dragging the thing out?"

"I want to do it my way."

I said nothing.

Denton got to his feet. He looked as dazed as though someone had thrown a bucket of cold water in his face. "How's that?" he asked.

The officer took charge of the situation. "Your boss has been murdered. Now, what are *you* doing?"

"I'm typing some records that he sent out to be transcribed."

"All right," the officer said. "Take it easy for a minute until Sergeant Sellers gets back. He's in charge. We're going to want all those records transcribed, and then we're going to want the original records so we can check the transcription.…What's on them?"

"Some data about exploration in Borneo."

"Okay. There may be a clue in that stuff. When did you get the records?"

"This morning."

"Who gave them to you?"

"Mr. Olney."

The officer turned to Olney. "Where did you get them?"

"Mr. Crockett gave them to me yesterday afternoon when he came out from his study. He told me to get in touch with Denton and be sure that the material was transcribed today."

"Then what?"

"Then he went back to his study."

The officer said, "All right, you folks sit down here. Don't go anyplace, don't do anything."

He walked over to the door and looked through into the study where a photographer was taking pictures of the corpse and the fingerprint man was dusting the place for latent prints.

I could see the intermittent flashes of light reflected from exploding flash bulbs. The officer started out by casually watching what was going on in the other room, then became interested.

Phyllis Crockett swayed close to me, put her hand on my arm. "Mr. Lam, I want you to protect me."

"From what?" I asked.

"From a false charge of murder."

Melvin Olney moved over to look past the officer's shoulder into the interior of the room, trying to see what was going on. Denton seemed still in a daze. He had seated himself and was running the fingers of his right hand through his hair as though trying to convince himself he was awake.

I said, "That's going to cost you money, Mrs. Crockett."

"I've got money."

"Do you think they can make out a case against you?"

"Yes."

"Why?"

"I've been framed."

"How do you know?"

"I'm beginning to put two and two together now. The whole thing adds up."

"Who framed you?"

"That," she said, "is your job. I've got the money. That's all I'm going to furnish. You're going to have to furnish the brains, the ability, the experience and the energy."

"Get a lawyer," I told her. "We'll work with the lawyer."

"I don't want a lawyer. For certain reasons, I can't afford to get one."

"Why?"

"It would make me look guilty."

The officer in the doorway turned to look back over his shoulder, saw Olney trying to get a glimpse at what was going on, and said, "Hey, get back there and sit down."

"Can't I look?" Olney asked.

The officer gave it to him straight from the shoulder. "No," he said, "you can't look."

I got Phyllis Crockett off to one side. "Why can't you go to a lawyer?" I asked in a low voice.

She shook her head.

"Tell me," I said in a half whisper. "I have to know what I'm up against if I'm going to do you any good."

"It's a long story," she said. "Very shortly after our marriage I realized that my husband didn't think marriage made any difference as far as his playing around was concerned....I'm impulsive and affectionate and...well, you know that, Donald."

She looked at me pleadingly.

"All right," I said, "I know that. So what?"

"Well, I get attracted to people and...well, Dean had some very old-fashioned ideas. He thought it was all right for him to play around but it was terrible if I even looked at anybody.... The last three months of our married life have been simply hell."

"Why didn't you divorce the guy?"

"He held the whip hand all the way along the line—do you understand what I mean, Donald? The whip hand."

"What about his will?" I asked. "Do you profit by his death?"

She shook her head.

"Do you know?"

"Well, I don't *know*, but I do know Dean told me that if I ever sued for divorce he could keep me from getting a divorce, he could keep me from getting a dime of alimony, and when he died it wouldn't do me a bit of good....Aside from that streak in his character, he wasn't too bad, but he was...he had that ego and—"

The door opened, and Frank Sellers and Inspector Thad Giddings entered the room.

"All right, folks," Sellers said, "let's answer a few questions. Mrs. Crockett, I'm going to begin with you."

She turned toward him.

"Ever see these before?"

Sellers held out his hand. In a plastic tray in the hand there were three darts.

"Why, I've seen—"

I nudged her with my elbow.

"I've seen some darts that looked like those," she said. "But of course I can't tell one dart from another."

Sellers glanced at me suspiciously, said, "Just move over there to that chair, Lam. Sit down over there. I'm coming to you in a moment. Right now I'm talking to Mrs. Crockett."

Inspector Giddings moved forward. "Step this way, Mrs. Crockett," he said.

Phyllis moved over toward the inspector and Sellers.

"Take a good look at those darts," Sellers said.

She looked at the darts closely.

"Well?" Sellers asked.

"I've told you all I can say," she said with an air of helplessness. "They look like darts that I've seen in my husband's collection, but I don't know how you can tell one dart from another."

"We'll find some way of telling, all right," Sellers said. "What about this plastic dish?"

"I've seen one just like that," she said.

"Where?"

"Over in my studio. I have several of them over there. I use them to keep my paintbrushes in."

"All right," Sellers said. "Let's get down to brass tacks. You were over in your studio yesterday afternoon?"

"Yes."

"What time did you go over there?"

"I don't know exactly what time it was. I would say it was about…oh, say…well, perhaps half-past three in the afternoon."

"And you were alone when you went in?"

"Yes, I was alone when I went in, but I wasn't alone…that is, someone else was there."

"Who?" Sellers asked.

"My model."

"Who's that?"

"Sylvia Hadley."

"How did she get in?"

"She has a key."

"You have extra keys for your studio?"

"Yes, of course. I use models from time to time and I can't have models sitting around in the lobby of the apartment house in case I'm late. When I'm using a model on a picture, I give her the key and let her come in and sit down. She returns the key when she finishes working as a model."

"So Sylvia Hadley had a key?"

"Yes."

"Was Sylvia there when you got in yesterday?"

"Yes."

"You don't know how long she had been there?"

"She said just a few minutes."

"You don't *know* how long?"

"No."

"Now then," Sellers said, turning to me, "*you* were at that studio yesterday afternoon?"

"Right."

"What time?"

"A little after four-thirty…say, four-forty on a guess."

"How long did you stay?"

"Fifteen or twenty minutes."

"Would you say you were away at four-fifty-five, or by five o'clock?"

I said, "Make it five-fifteen and you can be sure of it."

"When was the last time anybody saw Dean Crockett alive?" Sellers asked.

"I know he was alive shortly before sometime between four and five-thirty," Melvin Olney said, "but that's as close as I can fix the time."

"How do you know he was alive at that time?"

"Because I saw him. That's when he gave me the records that Denton is transcribing."

"Where was he?"

"Right here in the office."

"How about the door to that closet?"

"It was open."

"How about the door from the closet to the inner study?"

Olney pursed his lips and thought for a moment, then shook his head. "I wouldn't want to tell you," he said, "not for sure. I *think* it was...no. I'm not going to make any guesses."

"When did Crockett go back into that apartment?"

"I don't know. It was shortly before I left."

"When did you leave?"

"I had an appointment at five-forty-five. I'm sorry I can't fix the time element any better than that, but I was away from here by five-forty because I was on time for my appointment."

"Where?"

"Downstairs."

"With who?"

Olney pursed his lips and said, "With *whom*?"

"With *who*?" Sellers asked. "Hell, you know who you had the appointment with."

"It was a young lady."

"All right. There are half a million young ladies floating around here. What's her name?"

"She's a newspaper reporter."

"What's her name?"

Olney took a deep breath, and said, "I think perhaps you misunderstand the situation. I had an appointment with her but she didn't keep it. I talked with a man instead."

"What man?"

"Jack Spencer. He's a sports writer for the *Sun-Telegram*."

"Well, why didn't you say so?"

"Because I...I wanted to be absolutely fair. I hadn't expected to see Mr. Spencer, but he was waiting for me in the lobby and told me that he'd been sent to cover the story in place of the young woman writer that I had expected to meet."

"Then what did you do?"

"I went out with Spencer and we were out until…oh, I guess ten-thirty, and then he left."

"You can account for your time from five-forty-five until ten-thirty?"

"Certainly."

"After ten-thirty, what?"

"I went home."

"Directly home?"

"No, not directly."

"You're being rather cagey," Sellers said.

Olney shrugged his shoulders.

Sellers turned to Denton. "How about you? Where were you yesterday?"

"I wasn't feeling well. I kept quiet all afternoon and evening."

"What do you mean by keeping quiet?"

"I stayed in my apartment and caught up on some reading."

"In your apartment all by yourself?"

"Yes."

"Who else was around yesterday afternoon?" Sellers asked.

"Lionel Palmer," Olney said.

"Who's he?"

"He's the photographer who has charge of taking all of the pictures on Mr. Crockett's expeditions."

"Where do I find him?"

"He has a photographic studio and darkroom in one of the loft buildings."

"Whereabout?"

"At 92 East Rush—Rush is a short street that is only a couple of blocks long. It turns off—"

"I know the place," Sellers said. "What was he doing here?"

"He came up to discuss some photographs with Mr. Crockett."

"What sort of photographs?"

"I believe," Olney said, "that you better get the story of that from Lionel Palmer himself. As I understood it, Mr. Lam had asked for or had been given some photographs. Lionel wanted to be sure it was all right to cooperate with Mr. Lam."

"You mean Donald Lam, this guy here?"

Olney nodded.

"What did he want the pictures for?"

"I believe it was so he could get a clue as to who had stolen the blowgun and the jade statue. You had better ask Mr. Lam. All I know I got secondhand from Lionel Palmer."

Sellers looked at me, "You sure as hell get around," he said.

I said nothing.

"What did Crockett tell Palmer?" Sellers asked Olney.

"All I know is that I heard Lionel Palmer ask Mr. Crockett about furnishing some prints of pictures to Mr. Lam."

"And what did Crockett say?"

"Crockett laughed and told him not to be a damn fool, that Lam was his detective and was entitled to any cooperation he wanted."

"Anything else?"

"Yes. Mr. Palmer wanted to know just what Lam was doing, and Mr. Crockett explained that Lam had been hired by him to find out who had stolen a blowgun and a carved jade idol which had disappeared from the penthouse here the night before, during a party."

"And what was said next?"

"Lionel seemed upset. He grabbed Mr. Crockett by the coat lapel and said, 'Now, look here, Mr. Crockett, I want to know, am I trusted or am I not? If I'm under suspicion and you hired detectives to start checking up on me, I want to know it.'"

"Then what?" Sellers asked.

"Crockett doesn't like to be touched—I mean, he didn't like to be touched. It's hard to think of his being dead."

"Never mind all the verbs and syntax and grammar and what the hell," Sellers said. "We're after facts. What I want to know is what Crockett did."

"He put his hand in the middle of Lionel's chest and pushed him back."

"Hard?" Sellers asked.

"Pretty hard."

"What did he say?"

"He said, 'Damn you! Don't ever grab hold of my coat. Don't ever start pulling and hauling at me. Don't touch me. I hate to be touched. You know that.'"

"Then what?"

"Then he turned to me and told me once more that he wanted me to be sure to get hold of Wilbur Denton and have him here ready to start transcribing these records early in the morning, and...well, he sort of ignored Palmer."

"What did Palmer do?"

"He...well, he went into the other room."

"How did he act? Sullen? Angry?"

"Angry and sullen, I guess. I don't know. I never have been able to figure Lionel too well. He's rather emotional, and I can't tell just how he does feel."

"But he went out before you left?"

"No. He went into the transcribing office. He was there when I left—but Mr. Crockett had gone back to his own study and closed the door."

"You went out by five-forty-five?"

"Shortly before. I was down in the lobby by five-forty, per-haps a couple of minutes before that...but Mr. Crockett was back in his study before that. Perhaps you'd better let me explain. I know approximately when I came and when I left. I was here over an hour in all, but I can't reconstruct the event sequence to help you very much on the time element. I was

working on a lot of things, making a lot of calls while I was
waiting for Mr. Crockett to come out of his study. I can't recall
the exact time everything happened, but I know it was all
between four and five-thirty."

Sellers whirled to Mrs. Crockett. "How long did you remain
in your studio?" he asked. "Let's say Donald Lam left around
five o'clock. How long did you stay there after he left?"

"Perhaps another hour."

"Then you went out?"

"Yes."

"The model with you?"

"Yes."

"Where were you after that?"

"I came up here."

"Have dinner here?"

"Yes."

"Who else was here?"

"No one. I was here alone...that is, my husband was in the
penthouse here but he was closeted in his private apartment.
No one ever disturbs him in there."

"But there was an extra key to those doors? You could get in
there if you had to?"

"Yes. I opened the doors this morning."

"You knew there was an emergency key?"

"Naturally."

"You knew where it was kept?"

"Yes."

"Where?"

"In the safe."

"Who had the combination to that safe?"

"My husband and myself."

"No one else?"

"As far as I know, no one else."

"And you were here alone?"

"Yes."

"Your husband didn't open the door and come out?"

"No."

"How long were you here?"

"All evening."

"What did you do?"

"I watched television for a while, then I read and then went to bed."

"You and your husband have the same bedroom?"

"Yes. There's one bedroom with twin beds."

"You don't occupy the same bed?"

"No."

"How about the beds? Were they made up this morning?"

"Certainly."

"Who makes them up?"

"We have a maid service by the day."

"You didn't have any company last night?"

"No."

"You were here all alone?"

"Yes."

Sellers thought things over, said, "Okay. I guess we'll talk with this Lionel Palmer…I don't suppose by any chance *he* was . doing any modeling for you, was he?"

"No."

"You know him?"

"Of course."

"He's taken photographs of you?"

"Certainly. Hundreds of them."

"But he didn't have any key to your studio over there?"

She started to answer, then checked herself.

Sellers' eyes snapped to attention. "He had a key?"

"He has one at the moment, yes."

"Did he have one yesterday?"

"Yes."

"Why?"

"I was having him photograph some of my paintings."

"What's the idea?"

"You can't carry paintings around with you," she said. "I have him make photographic copies of my paintings on four-by-five colored film. Then, when I want to show someone my paintings without going to the bother of going over to the studio and getting the canvases out, I simply take this collection of four-by-five colored transparencies and I can discuss the pictures."

"How many photographs has he made?"

"I've painted something over two dozen pictures. He has colored films of all those. Those photos were made over a period of time. There were two new pictures he hadn't photographed as yet and I wanted those photographed. I...I presume he made the photographs sometime yesterday. That's when I told him to make them."

"What time?"

"I didn't give him any time. I saw him the night of the party and gave him the key to my study and told him to go in there whenever it was convenient to photograph the pictures, but I told him to phone to be certain I wasn't working, because if I was, I didn't want to be disturbed."

"You described the paintings you wanted photographed to him?"

"Yes. They were both on easels."

"You don't know whether he went over and photographed the paintings or not?"

"No."

"Well, we're getting around," Sellers said. "This is just a

preliminary talk. You people are going to be interrogated in more detail later."

Denton cleared his throat and said, "If you are interested in tracing all the keys to Mrs. Crockett's studio, I have extra keys in my desk."

"You have what?"

"Extra keys."

Mrs. Crockett hastened to explain. "Whenever I want some model to go in there, in case it is not convenient for me to meet her and give her a key before she arrives, I instruct her to come up here to get a key. Then I'll telephone Mr. Denton and tell him to give the girl a key."

"How many keys have you got?" Sellers asked Denton.

"Two."

"Where are they?"

"In my desk drawer."

"Take a look," Sellers said.

Denton went over to the desk drawer, said, "I keep them in this little stamp box."

He opened the drawer, then opened the box and stood frowning down at it.

"Only one key here," Sellers said.

"Yes," Denton admitted.

"There should be two?"

"There were two the last time I looked."

"When was that?"

"Day before yesterday."

"And there should be two?"

"I would say yes."

"Well, then, go ahead and say it."

"Yes."

"You keep this desk locked?" Sellers asked.

"No."

"Well, what do you know!" Sellers said. "One key missing. You're sure both of them were here a couple of days ago?"

"Yes, sir."

"*You* didn't give one to anyone?"

"No, sir."

"Okay," Sellers said. "There's no question but what Crockett was killed by somebody that shot a dart into his chest from that studio apartment over there across the light well. Probably the blowgun was fired through the bathroom window."

He turned to Inspector Giddings and said, "Get a bunch of men, Inspector. Start making inquiries of all persons who have apartments here in the place. See if anyone noticed a blowgun pointing out of the bathroom window. If so, find out what time it was and see if they had any opportunity to see the face of the person using the blowgun.

"That's all for now. I'm not going to detain you any longer at this time. Now, I don't want anybody to go near that door to the office there. In fact, you folks had all better get back in the other room. We're going to have officers coming and going in here and there'll be some newspapermen on the job any minute now. You folks can do what you please about talking to the newspaper people. As far as I'm concerned, there's nothing the police want to hush up about this."

"I am free to tell them about the missing key?" Denton asked.

"You're free to tell anybody anything you damn please," Sellers said. "Now, you can go on about your business. We're going to go to work."

Chapter Thirteen

I walked into the Cool & Lam offices, and Lionel Palmer jumped up from a seat back of the filing case where he had evidently been talking with Eva Ennis. Her face was slightly flushed and she was smiling in that peculiarly self-conscious but tolerant way a girl has when somebody has been handing her a pretty good line.

Palmer came striding across the office toward me.

"Hello, Palmer," I said.

"What the hell!" he stormed at me. "What was the idea of putting me on the spot with Dean Crockett?"

"Did I put you on a spot?"

"You know damn well you did. As soon as you were hired to get those stolen articles back, you made a beeline for my shop. That makes it look as if you felt I'd been mixed up in the theft. Crockett thinks so, and Olney thinks so. You know, I should smack you right in the kisser and teach you a lesson."

I took out my cigarette case, opened it, extended it to him. "Cigarette?" I asked.

"To hell with you," he said.

I took a cigarette, put it in my mouth, lit a match, and said, "What difference does it make whether I wanted to start out by looking at pictures or by looking at people?"

I saw that Eva Ennis had been edging up, looking at Lionel Palmer with the admiration which a girl of a certain type shows for a man who is talking big.

"Hell," he said, "you pumped me for all the dope on my friends. You've caused me so much trouble I think I'll just take it out of your hide in installments, and—"

I said, "You don't even know what trouble is—yet."

He said sneeringly, "I suppose *you're* going to make trouble for me?"

"Not me," I told him, "somebody else."

"Who?" he asked, noticing Eva Ennis out of the corner of his eye and getting his chin up and his chest stuck way out.

"The police," I told him.

It took a minute for that to dawn on him. Then his chest began to go down like a tire with a slow leak. "What the hell have the police got to do with it?"

"Quite a few things," I said. "They're looking for you now."

"For what?"

"They want to interrogate you."

"What the hell do they want to interrogate me about?"

I said, "Did you know that a blowgun and a small jade idol had been stolen from Crockett's house the night of the shindig?"

"Of course I knew it."

"It doesn't mean anything to you?"

"Why should it?"

"You knew a blowgun was missing?"

"Of course I did, I tell you. There's no secret about that. Crockett was yelling his head off about it. Yesterday afternoon he told me that he'd hired you and your partner to get the stuff back, and wanted to know why you were hanging around my place, and did I know—"

"I got the stuff back," I interrupted.

"So what? Why tell *me* about it?"

"I thought you might be interested."

"I'm not. I'm not interested in anything about you, or what you do, just so you don't ever stick your nose in my place again."

"The police are going to ask you some questions."

"Let them. I'll answer them."

"And the police are going to want to know what you were doing in Phyllis Crockett's studio apartment."

He was still talking big, but his chest was getting smaller by the minute. "What do you mean, Phyllis Crockett's studio apartment?"

"You have a key to it, I believe."

He didn't say anything to that.

"And you were in there sometime yesterday?"

"I don't have to account to *you* for what I do."

"That's entirely correct," I told him. "*You* don't and *I'm* not asking. I'm simply telling you that the police *are* going to be asking, and you will have to account to *them*."

"I had business in that apartment."

"Sure, sure," I said, "and you had a key to it and it was from that apartment that Dean Crockett was murdered."

He stepped back a couple of paces and his eyes became big. "Was what?"

"Murdered."

"What the hell are you talking about?"

"And," I said, "shortly before his murder, you had an interview with him in which you took hold of the lapel of his coat and he put his palm against your chest and pushed you halfway across the office and told you he was getting fed up with your familiarity both with himself and his wife.…The police are going to be very much interested in what you did after that time, because it was shortly after that that Crockett was murdered.… Now, if you'll excuse me, I have some work to do."

I left him standing there and walked over to my private office. As I opened the door, I glanced back at him and saw that he was looking at me with an expression of worried concern stamped all over his face.

Eva Ennis was watching him but there was no longer the

rapt admiration in her eyes that a doe gives to a buck who is winning a battle.

I stood with my hand on the doorknob, the door half-open, watching to see what would happen.

Eva turned away from Palmer and walked directly back to the filing case and began working on the files.

I went in, said hello to Elsie Brand, walked on back to my desk and seated myself.

Elsie said, "Bertha has been screaming her head off."

"Let her scream. The phone will ring pretty quick. The receptionist will tell you a Lionel Palmer wants to see me. Have her tell him to sit down and wait."

"The psychological approach?"

"That's right. I want him to cool his heels for a while."

"What about Bertha?"

I glanced at my watch and said, "Okay, give Bertha a ring."

"She wanted you to come in as soon as you arrived."

"Give her a ring."

Elsie gave Bertha a ring and nodded to me. I picked up my desk phone, said, "Hello, Bertha. I'm back."

"Back?" Bertha screamed at me. "Where the hell do you go these days? I come up to the office and try to find you, and no one knows where you are. You haven't even been in. You act like a corporation president on a vacation. This is a working organization. We've got business to do."

"What kind of business?"

"Come in here and I'll tell you."

"I can't," I said. "I have a man waiting in the office."

"Let him wait," Bertha said.

"That's what I intend to do," I told her, and hung up.

As soon as I hung up the phone, the receptionist called. "Mr. Lionel Palmer wants to see you."

"Tell him to wait. I'm busy."

I settled back in the swivel chair, put my feet on the desk and blew smoke at the ceiling. Within about five seconds the door burst open as though it was being taken off its hinges, and Bertha Cool came barging in.

"You listen to me!" she yelled, her face choleric with indignation. "We've got a job to do, and nobody knows what the hell *you're* doing. Somebody's got to prepare a report. I promised Crockett we'd give him daily reports."

"That's nice," I said.

"What have you done about returning that blowgun and the jade idol?"

"I have the jade idol," I said, opening a drawer in the desk, taking the idol out and putting it on the blotter.

"What about the blowgun?"

"The police have that now."

"Well," Bertha said, "it's about time you— The *police*?"

"The police."

"What the hell are the police doing?"

"Your friend, Frank Sellers, was interested in the blowgun the last I saw of it."

"Frank Sellers? He's with Homicide."

"That's right."

"What the hell was he doing when he saw you?" Bertha asked.

"Investigating a homicide."

"What homicide?"

"Your client," I said.

"Who do you mean?"

"Dean Crockett."

"You mean that he's been…that he's dead?"

"Dead as a doornail."

"Who killed him?"

"They don't know."

"What was he killed with?"

"There," I said, "is where we were a little too efficient, Bertha. Someone killed him with the blowgun that we recovered. At least, that's the way things look at the moment and that's what Frank Sellers thinks."

Bertha kept blinking her eyes at me as though she was biting the information off in chunks with her eyelids so as to help her brain digest it.

"When was he killed?" Bertha asked.

"Sometime last night. The body wasn't found until this morning."

"What angle are *you* working on?" Bertha Cool asked.

"The murder."

"Who for?"

"The widow."

"Why?"

"She's probably going to be accused of it."

"Did she do it?"

"I don't know."

"What does Sellers think?"

"He hasn't said."

She said, "Look here, Donald Lam, if Frank Sellers gets the idea that Mrs. Crockett killed her husband, and you stick your neck out trying to save Mrs. Crockett, it's going to make trouble."

"For whom?"

"For you. For the agency."

"Everybody makes trouble for me."

"I don't like it," Bertha said.

"Mrs. Crockett," I told her, "doesn't like it either."

"What about dough?"

"I haven't asked her."

"Well, you ask her," Bertha said. "Get her in here. I'll ask her. That's the trouble with you, Donald Lam. You're one of these easygoing, good-natured guys that believes everyone....I've told you a thousand times that whenever you take on any sort of a job you're to get a retainer, get some money in advance. They may take this woman and throw her in the can. Then they may convict her of murder and she can't inherit a cent. Then we'll be holding the bag."

"That's right," I said. "Therefore, we shouldn't let her get convicted of her husband's murder."

"*Always* get dough in advance," Bertha said, "then you don't care what happens."

"How much did *you* get out of Dean Crockett?"

Bertha tried to be dignified. "With a man of that caliber you can't— What the hell are you trying to do, you little bastard? Are you trying to bait me?"

"I was just wondering," I said. "You said *always* get dough in advance."

"Well, that's a different situation."

"Why is it different?"

"He's a millionaire. He's good for anything he orders."

"He isn't good for anything now."

Bertha sucked in a deep breath, started to say something, then turned and stormed out of the office.

I waited another five minutes, then told Elsie Brand to advise the receptionist that Lionel Palmer could come in now.

He looked a lot different by the time he got into the office. He'd lost all of his belligerent, aggressive superiority.

"Look, Lam," he said, "I want to know exactly what it is the police have got on me. Just what—"

He broke off and his eyes grew big as he saw the jade Buddha sitting in the middle of the blotter on my desk. "What...what's that?"

"The missing jade Buddha," I said casually.

"You...you recovered it?"

"It didn't walk in here under its own power."

"Where did you get it?"

"Oh, I recovered it."

"When?"

"Yesterday."

"Where?"

"From the person who had it."

"Look here, Lam, I have a reason for asking. I want to know who had that Buddha."

"You did," I said, and lit another cigarette.

He started to jump up out of his chair with a big show of indignation, then thought better of it and said, "What the hell are you talking about?"

"I'm talking about you and the jade Buddha."

"You didn't recover it from me."

"I recovered it from one of your cameras. It was wrapped in cotton and put in your Speed Graphic—the one with the wide-angle lens."

"You're crazy."

"It's a debatable point," I said. "Bertha Cool, my partner, agrees with you at times, so I'm not going to argue against a majority opinion….Nevertheless, that's where I recovered the jade Buddha."

"I don't believe you."

"You don't have to. Frank Sellers will."

"Who's Frank Sellers?"

"The tough cop on Homicide who is going to be giving you a working over."

"Does he know it?"

"Know what?"

"That you recovered…that you *said* you recovered this Buddha in the back of one of my cameras?"

"Not yet."

"You're going to tell him?"

"Sure."

Palmer began to squirm around in his seat. "Look here, Lam," he said, "you're a pretty damn good fellow."

"Thanks."

"There's no reason why you and I shouldn't get along."

"None whatever."

"How do you suppose that jade Buddha got inside of my camera?"

"I wouldn't know. It's not my business to know. That's up to Sellers. That's what the taxpayers pay him for. He'll find out."

"You…you think he will?"

"I know damn well he will."

Palmer got nervous again and started hitching his chair up close to mine. He lowered his voice, looked through the half-open door to Elsie Brand's office, where she was sitting checking some papers and pretending not to listen.

"Now, look, Donald, we can do business."

I raised my eyebrows.

"I'll tell you what I *think* happened."

"Go ahead."

"But I'll want you to protect my confidence."

I said, "I'm working for a client. I protect nobody on anything except my client. My client's the one I protect, and the only one I protect."

"But you could…you could…you have to protect your sources of information."

I stretched my fists back up over my head, yawned, and said, "I don't need any sources of information. I can get all I need. What did Sylvia Hadley say when she came up to your studio and found the jade idol gone?"

"Sylvia!" he exclaimed.

I nodded.

"It…it couldn't have been Sylvia."

"What makes you think it couldn't?"

"Why, she…she—"

"She was up to your studio yesterday afternoon, wasn't she?"

"She dropped in briefly before she went up to Mrs. Crockett's to pose as a model."

"Uh-huh."

"But she's all right. She's on the up-and-up."

"Make an excuse to be left alone in your outer room there? The one where you keep your cameras?"

"She was alone there. She didn't need to make any excuse. I was in the darkroom doing some work. She was in there with me for a while and then the fumes of the acid fixing bath bothered her a little so she went outside and waited for me out there."

"And after she looked in the camera and found the jade idol was gone, did you notice a change in her manner?"

He looked at me as though I'd socked him in the solar plexus.

"Well," I said, getting up and stretching, "I've got to leave now. Come in any time."

I walked across through Elsie Brand's office and opened the door.

Lionel Palmer walked out like a man in a daze. His sports jacket seemed two sizes too big for him.

Eva Ennis watched him go. There was a puzzled expression on her face.

I started back to the office, and Eva Ennis brought over some papers from the files. "These are the papers that you asked for the other day, Mr. Lam. You wanted the affidavits in the Smith case."

"Oh, yes," I said, taking the papers.

She looked at me with seductive eyes.

"What did you do to him?" she asked.

"Who?"

She nodded her head toward the door. "Lionel Palmer."

I assumed surprise. "Nothing. Why?"

"He seemed so…so deflated."

"Did he? I didn't notice."

"He was waiting for you to come in. He said he was going to…well, he made threats."

"Did he?"

"He was going to mop up the office floor with you."

"Is that so? How long have you been working here, Eva?"

"Just around two months."

"When you've been here longer," I said, "you'll learn to take those things in your stride. Mopping up the office floor with me doesn't entitle a guy to anything—least of all a pleasant look from the filing clerk.…What did Palmer want?"

"What do you mean?"

"You know what I mean. What did he want?"

"Oh," she said self-consciously, "he wanted…well, he wanted… he wanted—period. Do I have to express it any plainer than that?"

"A lot plainer," I told her. "I'm not talking about your body. I'm talking about our files."

"Why," she said in surprise, "he didn't want anything out of the files."

"I thought he did, the way he was standing around by you over there at that filing drawer."

"Why, no, he was just…well, you know, talking…making a play."

She waited a minute, then giggled and said, "A preliminary."

"I thought he was interested in the files."

"Oh, he was just making conversation on that."

"What kind of conversation?"

"A build-up."

"Do you remember just what he said?"

"Oh, he asked me about the filing system and asked me about how long I'd been here, and how a system could be arranged in an office of this size so that one girl could find things after another girl had quit, and—"

"And he asked you to show him a filing drawer?"

She shifted her position seductively and said, "He wanted to get me over there in the corner."

"For what?"

"Be your age," she said archly.

"Did he have restless hands?"

"*All* men have restless hands."

"And did he ask you to show him the filing drawer?"

"Yes."

"Did he open the drawer or did you?"

"He did."

"And was it the drawer that had the C files in it?"

She frowned thoughtfully and said, "Why...I guess it was. I didn't really notice."

"Have you made a file on Dean Crockett?"

"Yes."

"What's in it?"

"Just Mrs. Cool's notes about guarding the place and preventing theft of curios."

"If he comes back," I said, "keep him away from the filing cabinet."

"Oh, *he* isn't coming back," she said.

"You can't tell," I told her.

"Mr. Lam," she said impulsively, "I think you're just wonderful!"

"Yes?"

"Yes."

"Why?"

"You're so...so utterly fearless."

"I'm not fearless," I told her, "I'm just resigned."

The door of my private office opened, and Elsie Brand came out. I saw her look around for me and for a moment she didn't spot me.

Eva Ennis was standing very close to me. She was looking up in my eyes with an expression of extreme feminine approval. She was about to say something when Elsie spotted me.

Elsie came over and said quietly, "I'm very sorry to interrupt you, but there's a young woman on the line who has to talk with you, Donald. She says it's very important."

"Give her name?"

"No."

"Okay," I said.

I gave Eva Ennis a smile which she could interpret as a promise that I'd be back to resume the conversation at some future date.

Elsie Brand walked beside me as I went toward the office.

"I'll have to send her a copy of the game laws," I said.

"The girl on the telephone?"

"Eva Ennis."

"Why the game laws?"

"I want her to learn something about open seasons, poaching on private property, and getting a hunting license."

I grinned and picked up the telephone.

A frightened feminine voice said, "Donald, I have to see you right away."

"Who is this?"

"Sylvia Hadley."

"What's happened?" I asked.

"Lots of things are *going* to happen. I hope you can get here before they start happening."

"Where's here?"

"My apartment."

"Where?"

"Cresta Vista, Apartment 319. Will you come?"

"I don't know," I said. "It depends on what it's all about. I'm working on a case and my time belongs to my client."

"Donald, please, please, *please* come," she said. "It's important, both to me and to you. It…it's terribly important to Phyllis."

I hesitated just long enough to let her know I wasn't eager, then said, "Very well. I'll be up."

"Just as quickly as possible, please, Donald."

"Okay," I said, and hung up.

I said to Elsie, "I'm going to be out for an hour or so in case anyone wants me."

"Be careful," Elsie said.

"Why careful?" I asked.

"Because I know you can't be good," she told me.

Chapter Fourteen

I pushed the mother-of-pearl button on the side of the door at 319 and Sylvia called through the door, "Who is it?"

"Lam," I said.

She flung the door open. "Oh, Donald!" she said. "Donald, I'm so glad you came!"

Her hands were on my arm, the fingers gripping, her eyes looking into mine, her lips half-parted. "Oh, Donald," she said, "this is terrible. It's absolutely terrible."

"All right," I told her, "let's get down to brass tacks. Tell me what's so terrible about it."

She closed the door and turned the bolt. "Come over here, Donald," she said, "and sit down."

She led the way to a davenport, sat down, kicked her shoes off, doubled up her legs so the tightly stretched expanse of nylon stockings was visible, and sat very close to me, her hands with interlaced fingers resting on my shoulder. "Donald," she said, "it's terrible. I don't want to tell you, but I have to."

"All right, go on. Tell me," I said.

"That jade idol."

"What about it?"

"I took it."

"Uh-huh," I said. "Mind if I smoke?"

"Donald, I don't believe you're paying any attention to me at all."

"Of course I am. You took the jade idol. Mind if I smoke?"

"No," she pouted.

"Want one?"

She hesitated, then said, "All right."

I gave her one of my cigarettes and held my lighter. She leaned forward for the light, holding my hand with one of hers, her eyes looking up from the flame to my face. "Donald, I need your help. I need it so terribly, terribly much."

"Go on," I said, "you stole the jade idol. What happened?"

"Donald, I can tell from the way you're acting you don't believe me."

"I believe you stole the jade idol."

"Well, then, why are you so…so sort of casual about the whole thing?"

"What do you want me to do, drop down on the floor and throw a fit? You stole the jade idol. You've decided to tell me about it now because you know that I found out you had stolen the idol and the method you used to smuggle it out of the apartment."

"No, no, Donald, I swear that's not true! If you'll only listen. If you'll only let me tell you the whole story."

"Go on," I said. "You wanted me to get out here in a hurry. You acted as though you didn't have much time."

"I'm afraid I don't."

"Better use what you have then."

She squirmed around, getting a little closer to me. The skirt slipped back over the tightly stretched stockings, exposing the upper part of her legs, her lips were within inches of my ear.

"Donald," she said, "I was disloyal to my friend."

"What friend?"

"Phyllis."

"How were you disloyal?"

"I did things with…with her husband."

"What sort of things?"

She hesitated and said, "Well, for one thing, he wanted me to participate in a scheme, a plot."

"What sort of a plot?"

"I don't know, but he had something all planned out. He was a deep thinker and whatever it was he had planned was part of a carefully thought-out scheme."

"What did he want you to do?"

"He wanted me to steal the idol."

"Oh," I said, "that's it. Your defense now is that you took the idol because he asked you to. Is that it?"

"Of course, Donald. That's what I'm telling you—what I'm trying to tell you."

"Well, you've told me."

"No, I haven't. I've just told you the naked facts."

"And now you want to dress them up?"

"Nudity is interesting," she said, "but nakedness is not artistic."

"All right," I said, "you object to nakedness. Go ahead and dress up the facts."

"Donald, I have an idea that you're condemning me in advance, without hearing what I have to say."

"I'm trying to hear what you have to say."

"Well, you're not making it easy for me."

"What do you want me to do?"

"Be sympathetic. I— Oh, Donald, I feel terribly alone and helpless. I just want to have some strong man to…to take me and protect me."

"I'm not strong."

"Yes, you are, Donald. You're wonderful, only you don't know it."

"Is this part of the naked truth?" I asked. "Or part of the dressing?"

"I do believe you're trying to be nasty," she said, and tried to shake me, but wound up by shaking herself, her body moving back and forth against mine.

I leaned forward and reached for an ashtray.

She took a deep breath. "It was like this," she said. "Dean Crockett came to me and told me that he wanted to arrange a theft on the night of that party. He said that he wanted to have the second of the two jade Buddhas disappear."

"Why?"

"He wanted an excuse to hire detectives."

"Why?"

"That's something I don't know."

"Suppose you tell me just what Dean Crockett told you."

"He told me that he was very anxious to have it appear that some thief had stolen the second of the carved jade Buddhas from his collection. *One* of the jade Buddhas had been stolen about three weeks ago. He said he was going to hire a detective to protect his study. He had also put an X-ray arrangement in the elevator so that he could turn this X-ray on."

"Simply to keep people from stealing things?" I asked.

She said, "I gathered that had been put in for another purpose."

"What?"

"So that people entering the apartment could be X-rayed to see if they were carrying any weapons. As soon as a person entered the elevator, the X-ray machine was turned on and a fluoroscope picked up the image. There was some kind of an arrangement by which the image on the fluoroscope was projected on a screen above. I don't know whether it was done by mirrors or some sort of a special television circuit. Anyway, a person entering the elevator going either up or down could be studied all the way by someone watching in a little hidden compartment back of the elevator shaft."

"You're sure of this?"

"Oh, yes," she said, and laughed. "Talk about feeling naked. My Heavens, you should see a woman in that fluoroscope! You can see every bone in her body and the metal garter clasps and everything like that. It's the same system they have in prisons. Visitors in the high-security prisons, you know, have to be X-rayed. You stand in one of these booths and they study everything you have...." She giggled and said, "You should see a man in that fluoroscope if you *really* want to see something."

"How come?"

"Oh," she said, "men carry such an assortment of junk. You can see the cigarette cases, the coins in their pants pockets, fountain pens, tiepins, cuff links, everything."

"You've watched people go up and down in the elevator?"

"Yes."

"Why? Just for kicks?"

"No, I've worked for Mr. Crockett."

"What do you mean, worked?"

"Well, I've sat there on guard when he expected someone to call on him who might have a weapon. He'd have people monitor the persons going up and down in the elevator and sometimes I did that monitoring for him."

"You got to know him quite well?"

"*Real* well."

"So then he told you he wanted this jade Buddha stolen?"

"Yes."

"And he wanted that stolen so he could have an excuse to keep a detective on the job guarding the place?"

"Yes, that was part of it."

"What was the rest of it?"

"I don't know. That's what sort of worries me."

"And just what were you supposed to do?"

"Well, he was going to get this detective who would be hardboiled, and...well, she would— You see, it had to be a woman because he wanted her to be able to search women guests if it became necessary, and—"

"Wait a minute," I said. "Let's back up and take another look at that. Why did he want women guests searched?"

"To keep them from taking anything."

I shook my head.

"You don't think so?"

"I don't think so. Crockett was wealthy. If he had decided to search any woman guest, he could have really got in a tough spot."

"But not if the woman guest had something concealed on her that she was taking from the apartment."

"He'd have to catch her red-handed," I said. "He'd have to be absolutely certain of what he was doing, and—suppose the woman guest simply refused to be searched and put it up to him to call the police and lodge a charge, if he was going to carry things that far."

"Well, couldn't he do that?"

"He could have, but he wouldn't actually have done it."

"He told me he was going to get a woman who was so tough that nobody was going to talk her out of anything."

"He had the woman detective all picked?"

"Yes. Your partner, Bertha Cool."

"Then why did he want you to steal the jade Buddha?"

"I think, Donald, he was laying a foundation for something that was scheduled to happen the day after the party. I think that's why he wanted to be certain that something was missing.

"Anyway, he told me what to do. I was to wait until the coast was clear, then I was to smash the glass in the glass case which contained the remaining jade Buddha. I was to wrap it in cotton and put it in the back of the camera Lionel Palmer used for the group shots—the one with the wide-angle lens. Mr. Crockett told me that that camera would be used only once during the evening, and that would be to take a shot of the guests all assembled at the table. After that, he said Lionel wouldn't use it and it would be perfectly safe to put the jade Buddha in. You see, the X-ray was always turned off when Lionel Palmer went up and down because once they didn't do it and every picture Lionel took was all fogged. The X-rays simply ruined the film.

"I think that was the time that Lionel first found out about the X-ray machine in the elevator. He couldn't imagine what had happened to his films but he knew that there had been some kind of sabotage, so he went to Dean Crockett and told him that something had happened and that he rather suspected he'd been in front of an X-ray machine sometime during the evening."

"So then Crockett told him about the X-ray in the elevator?"

"I don't know whether he told him or not, but he did tell Lionel that he would look into the matter and if there was any truth to the charge he'd see that it didn't happen again. He talked vaguely about protective measures that had been installed by some detective agency and said he didn't know too much about them."

"All right," I said. "Dean Crockett told you to take the jade Buddha and put it in the camera. Then what?"

"Well, of course, Lionel would carry it out and then I was to drop in and see Lionel the next day and...well, Lionel had taken some publicity pictures of me and I was to come in for more pictures.

"Mr. Crockett said he would see that Lionel would be in the darkroom developing and printing pictures all day, making enlargements for publicity purposes. He said if I hung around a bit, I wouldn't have any difficulty getting to the shelf where the cameras were kept and taking the carved jade Buddha out. And then no one would ever know how it got out of his place."

"So what?"

"So you…big smart you, came along and figured out where the jade Buddha was and went and took it out of the back of Lionel's camera, and then you put somebody watching Lionel's studio so that when I showed up to try and get the Buddha out of the camera, you were able to put the finger on me."

"And you knew that?"

"I figured it out after a while."

"And why are you telling me all this now?"

"Because I'm frightened."

"Why?"

"Because Lionel is not going to back me up.…I'll be accused of stealing the jade Buddha. Before I realized the whole situation, I talked too much to Lionel, and he knows that I'm the one who put the jade Buddha in his camera, and the one who came to get it. Of course, when it was gone I accused Lionel of having found it and concealed it somewhere, and…I guess I've led with my chin."

"And?" I asked.

She stroked the side of my cheek with her fingertips, ran her fingers up into my hair and stroked the hair back gently. "And now," she said, "I seem to be more or less in your power because, with Dean Crockett gone, there's no one to back up my story and…I *could* be in a horrible fix unless you decided to help me out."

"Perhaps," I said, "it hasn't occurred to you that I am working on the case…and for a client."

"Of course it has. That's why I wanted to see you."

"I'm working for someone else, Sylvia."

"Of course. For Mrs. Crockett."

"Therefore, I'm not able to do anything for you."

"Donald, turn around and look at me," she said.

"I'm listening. I don't need to look."

"I want to look at you. I want you to look at me."

She placed her hand under my chin and gently but firmly pulled my head around to hers.

"Now, keep looking at me, Donald," she said. "I want you to know that I wouldn't have asked you to come here if I didn't feel that you needed me as much as I needed you."

"Why do I need you?" I asked.

"In order to protect Phyllis."

"And how are you going to help me protect Phyllis?"

"Because," she said, "I could forget about Phyllis going into the bathroom and closing the door and then hearing the window open, and…well, I got curious and I turned around and looked out of the window over my shoulder."

"Now," I said, "I presume that you want to tell me that you were able to see the bathroom window by looking over your shoulder."

"No, I couldn't see the bathroom window. I was standing on the modeling platform and that's near the bank of frosted-glass windows. Some of those windows swivel in and out for ventilation, not very far, just far enough to let the air in….They don't want to have them swing out far enough so that persons in other apartments can see in and observe what's happening because in that event…well, you know, they'd be looking in at the nude models—some people seem to think that it's a great novelty to see a woman with her clothes off."

"To some people it is."

"It doesn't need to be," she said gently. "After all, it's natural, Donald. What's wrong with nudity?"

"You're talking about a bathroom window," I said.

"Oh, yes. I looked over my shoulder and, of course, I couldn't see the bathroom window, but I could see out of the window through the little crack that was open, and— Donald, is it a crime to suppress evidence?"

"Yes."

"And if I told you I saw something significant and you kept it from the police it would be a crime?"

"I wouldn't have seen anything," I said.

"I know, but if I saw something and told you about it, and you told me to keep it from the police, then it might—"

"But I wouldn't tell you to keep it from the police."

"Not even if I saw the tip of a blowgun out of the bathroom window—saw it moving up and down like someone was taking aim?"

"Don't be silly," I said.

"I'm not being silly, Donald. I'm trying to be helpful."

"Why?"

"Because I want you to help me."

I said, "I'm sorry, Sylvia, but it's no dice."

Her eyes grew hard. "What do you mean, it's no dice? You mean you're going to throw me overboard?"

"*I'm* not going to throw you overboard."

"Are you going to let Phyllis?"

"How could Phyllis throw you overboard?"

"By keeping you all to herself."

"She doesn't have me all to herself."

"Your services, I mean."

"Just what did you want me to do?"

"To get Phyllis to remember that Dean Crockett told her in strict confidence that the theft of the little jade idol was to be a put-up job and that he had arranged for me to do it and that I was acting under his orders."

"Do you think he told her that?"

"Oh, I'm certain he did."

"Why are you so certain?"

"Because it would have been such a natural thing for him to have done, and…you know, he told Phyllis lots of things. If she only wants to cudgel her brains a little bit, she can remember."

"Suppose she doesn't?"

"Then that will be just too bad."

"For whom?"

"For her—perhaps for both of us. Donald, you simply *have* to stand back of me in this thing. Am I going to have to use my wiles on you?"

She was cuddled up as close as she could get now, holding my arm tight against her body.

"What do you think you're doing now?" I asked.

"Oh," she said, "I'm just commencing now. This is just a preliminary—do you want to see a real wile?"

"No," I told her. "Get the hell away from me for a minute and let me think."

She pouted. "Now, was that nice?"

I said, "You're a babe in the woods, an amateur. You just don't have any idea of what the police will do when the going gets tough. They'll take you to pieces."

"Well, suppose they do?" She looked up defiantly and said, "I guess I wasn't born yesterday. I know that I can get immunity for anything *I* did if I give them evidence that will help them in a murder case. The trouble is, I don't want to turn against Phyllis."

I pushed her away and got to my feet.

"Okay," I said, "try it and see where you come out."

"Donald!"

"You heard me."

"Aren't you going to be cooperative?"

"And find myself in the can for suborning perjury, and then get Phyllis into a spot where she loses her case before it even starts? Don't be funny. If you know anything, go tell it to the police. And remember this, when you do, they're going to take you to pieces."

"They are not," she said defiantly. "I'll get immunity."

She wiggled off the couch with a great show of legs and started toward me.

I walked over to the door, unbolted and opened it, went out and pulled the door shut behind me.

Just as the door was closing I heard her scream vindictively, "You sonofabitch!"

Chapter Fifteen

Phyllis Crockett answered the telephone.

"Donald Lam talking," I said. "I have to see you."

"When?"

"Now, if possible."

"Come on up," she invited.

"Where? The penthouse or the studio?"

"The studio," she said. "I've left word at the desk that you're to be admitted whenever you come up."

"How have things been?" I asked.

"All right."

"Rough?"

"Not too rough."

"They're going to get worse," I told her. "I'll be up."

I hung up the telephone, drove to the apartment house, and the clerk at the desk smiled at me as though I owned the place. I went on up to the twentieth floor and pressed the button on Mrs. Crockett's studio.

She was wearing a black strapless gown that showed lots of flesh. "Hello, Donald," she said. Her face looked drawn and taut.

"Where are you going in that?" I asked.

"In what?"

I pointed to the dress.

"Don't you like it?" she asked.

"That isn't the question," I said. "You're a widow, remember? You're supposed to be prostrated with grief."

"Phooey!" she said. "There's no use making a pretense like

that. Dean and I had been physically separated for more than a year and— Do you know what he did the day of his death?"

"What?"

"It seems he'd had his attorney prepare divorce papers earlier in the week. He telephoned his attorney to file the divorce papers the next morning."

"The attorney didn't do it?"

"There wasn't any next morning. He was dead."

"Do the police know that?"

"The police know it, the newspapers know it, everybody knows it."

"How do you know?"

"They've been hounding me to death—not the police so much as the reporters. I gave the police a straight story, and they're giving me a breathing spell."

"They're checking every angle of your story," I said. "If they find the least thing wrong with it, they'll come back at you hard."

"Well, they can't find anything wrong with it."

"What about the reporters?"

"They've been asking the most impertinent questions. I wouldn't see them at all. Melvin Olney has been worth his weight in gold.

"That's one thing about Melvin, Donald. He was loyal to Dean Crockett while Dean was alive, but he knew Dean's shortcomings just as well as anyone else. We had a nice talk after you left. He told me that he wanted to stay on, that his loyalty had been to Dean but that if I would let him stay on with me, his loyalty would be with me."

"Why should he stay on?"

"What do you mean?"

"What do you want with a press agent?"

"He's more than that, Donald, he's a manager. He handles things and sort of takes charge and knows the ropes. He's *really* done a job with the newspaper people. He's been courteous and considerate but he's kept them away from me."

"Have you been out?"

"No."

"When did the police get finished with this apartment?"

"About two hours ago. They told me they were finished and that I could go ahead and use it. I've been down here most of the time so that in case any of the newspaper men did get in they—"

"This place isn't so good," I said.

"Why not?"

"You can keep the reporters out of the penthouse but you can't keep them out of here."

"...I didn't care about having Melvin know that I was seeing you right now. I told him I was going down to the studio and try to get a little rest."

"He knows you're down here?"

"Yes."

I said, "I want you to think back to yesterday—the day of the murder."

"What about it?"

I said, "I called here in the afternoon and gave you that blow-gun."

"You didn't really give it to me, you left it here with me to be delivered to Dean."

"That's right. Now, I want to know what you did after I left."

"Painted."

"Did you go to the bathroom?"

"Why, Donald," she said. "How do I know? I'm a normal human being. I go to the bathroom once in a while and I can't remember two or three days later every trip I made to the john."

"You know what I mean," I said. "Did you go to the bathroom for some special purpose?"

She smiled and said, "If I went it must have been for a special purpose."

I said, "Sylvia Hadley says you went into the bathroom, closed the door, and were gone for some time. She says you pushed the blowgun out of the bathroom window. She heard the window being raised and saw the tip of the blowgun."

"She's a liar. She couldn't have seen it."

"You mean she's a liar because you didn't do it, or that she's a liar because she couldn't have seen it?"

"Both."

"Let's try an experiment," I said. "What do we have here that is about the length of that blowgun? What about a mop stick, or a broom if we come right down to it?"

"I have a brush with a long handle, but I don't see what you're trying to prove. Sylvia simply couldn't have seen a thing."

I said, "We'll talk about that in a minute. I want you to go in the bathroom, open the window and stick the handle of that long-handled brush out just as far as you can push it."

She started to say something, changed her mind, went to the closet, came out with the brush, walked into the bathroom and opened the bathroom window.

"Like this?" she asked.

"Like that," I said.

I walked over to the frosted-glass window, tilted the pane so the window was open about two inches, then went to the model stand, stood on it and looked back through the opening in the window.

I could see the last ten or twelve inches of the brush handle. I closed the window, said, "Okay. She could have seen it."

"She could have?"

I nodded.

She bit her lip.

"She'll be telling the police pretty quick," I said. "Now then, if you didn't kill your husband, you certainly have put yourself in quite a spot. If you did kill him, you've put yourself in the gas chamber."

"Donald, I didn't kill him."

"*Did* you open the window and push the blowgun out?"

Her eyes were downcast. "Yes," she admitted in a low voice.

"How come?"

"It was almost immediately after you left, Donald. I knew that my husband would want to know about the blowgun having been recovered. I remembered his window was open. I went to the bathroom and while I was in there I started thinking. I opened the window a crack to see if I could see him."

"Did you see him?"

"Yes."

"Where was he?"

"In that little closet where his body was found. He was standing right near the window. His back was turned toward me and he was talking with someone. I…I think it…I couldn't see who it was. It might even have been a woman."

"All right. What did you do?"

"Opened the window and called his name."

"Did he hear you?"

"No."

"Then what?"

"I called a second time and then pushed the blowgun out of the window so he could see it and hollered 'yoo hoo.'"

"Did he hear you?"

"No."

"What did you do?"

"I saw that he was talking with this person and that he was so completely preoccupied he wouldn't hear me call, so I pulled the blowgun in, stood it in the corner, closed the bathroom window and went back to go on with my painting."

"Why didn't you use the flashlight to attract his attention? You could have thrown a beam of light on the wall of that closet that would have attracted his attention."

"I just didn't think about it at the moment."

"Isn't that what you use that flashlight for?"

"Yes."

"Then you should have thought of it."

"But that would have attracted the attention of my husband's visitor and that might have interrupted something important. I didn't want to do that."

"Do you use that flashlight signal often?"

"No. Dean didn't want to be disturbed when he was in his study—I'd use the light to signal him only when I had something important—not just for chitchat."

"What about Sylvia?"

"What do you mean?"

"I want to know about her."

She said, "You've seen enough of her, you should know her."

"What do you mean by that?"

"You've seen all there is to see."

"Oh," I said, "is she like that?"

"Of course she's like that. She's completely uninhibited and like many women with really beautiful figures, she's an exhibitionist. She likes to show her body. She likes to have people pay attention to her."

"What people?"

"All people."

"Dean Crockett?"

She said wearily, "Oh, I suppose so. Although Dean at times could be completely preoccupied with his work and at those times he'd brush women to one side as though they were annoying distractions—I guess the way he looked at it, that's what they were."

"But you don't think he brushed Sylvia to one side?"

"I don't *think* he did. If Sylvia got her mind made up, she wouldn't brush off easily."

"You didn't care?"

"Would it have helped if I had?"

"Probably not, but what I'm getting at is whether you had any suspicions and if so why you kept on being so nice to Sylvia."

"What should I have done?"

"Lots of wives would have scratched her eyes out."

"If I scratched the eyes out of every woman Dean Crockett the Second had bedded, there'd be a lot of blind women groping their way through life."

"But I gathered you felt he was too preoccupied to—"

"Oh, he had his moments. When he'd snap out of it he was a fast worker."

"There were two jade Buddhas?"

"That's right."

"How was Sylvia fixed for money?"

"I don't know. I don't know anything at all about that part of her life. I do know she had some sources of supply. Not long ago she asked me to endorse a check so she could get it cashed. It was for a thousand dollars."

"Payable to her?"

"Yes."

"Who issued the check—do you know?"

"Yes. I looked at the signature—I had to, since I was actually guaranteeing the check. Sylvia didn't like it. She thought I was snooping. I laughed at her. I told her I wouldn't guarantee anyone's check without looking at the signature."

"Who had signed it?"

"Mortimer Jasper."

"Do you know him?"

"I've met him at art auctions."

"Is Sylvia a girl who appreciates beauty in art?"

"She appreciates beauty in her own figure and in her own mirror—but I like her, Donald."

"Why?"

"I don't know. She's so completely uninhibited, I guess."

"Suppose she was hard pressed for money for one reason or another. She had a chance to steal those carved jade Buddhas and sell them. Who could she have sold them to?"

Phyllis shook her head and said, "No, that's not like Sylvia. Sylvia at times can be a regular little tramp, but in money matters she'd be honest. She—" Abruptly she caught herself.

"Well?" I asked.

"Come to think of it," she said, "Sylvia has been acting strangely the last two or three weeks. The other day I saw her sitting in a sports car with Mortimer Jasper. They were parked downstairs. He'd evidently driven her to work and I...well, I just wondered at the time. They had their heads close together and were talking and—"

"Just who is Mortimer Jasper?" I asked.

"That depends on whom you ask."

"I'm asking you."

"Well, some people think he's a sportsman, a man about

town, a collector of unusual Oriental art, and some people think he's…"

"Go on," I said. "Some people think he's what?"

"Well, sort of a fence."

"Where would I find him?"

"He has a place, a little shop of sorts, down in the business district, but I don't know what his home address is. I guess you can find him in the phone book."

"Did you tell the police anything about trying to attract your husband's attention and holding the blowgun out the window and calling to him?"

"No."

"Why not?"

"I didn't think it was necessary."

"All right," I told her. "That's where you've put your neck in a noose. Now then, I want you to think pretty carefully. After I left, you went to the bathroom.…Did Sylvia go to the bathroom?"

"Heavens, I don't know, Donald. Everyone has to some time. We were here alone painting and… Yes, that's right. Wait a minute, she did."

"And the blowgun was in the bathroom?"

"Yes. I stood it right there in the corner."

"How long was she in the bathroom?"

"I don't know. I didn't time her. I went on with my painting and…to tell you the truth I was completely absorbed in what I was doing and didn't pay much attention to what happened, but I do remember she went to the bathroom because I was trying to get just the effect I wanted on the painting and I was having a little trouble with it. I wished she was back there on the modeling stand so I could see just the way the light was coming in. I remember that much very distinctly."

"When the police come back," I told her, "tell them that you're simply not able to answer any more questions today.

"Now then, get out of that dress and put on something quiet, conservative and indicative of sorrow."

"I don't feel any sorrow."

"Yes, you do," I told her, "and you're going to be sure the world knows how you feel. Your husband was not particularly close to you. He was a very strange character. He was always aloof. You never seemed to get to know him, but you respected him and you admired him from a distance. You put him on a pedestal.

"Unfortunately, he didn't care for women. He was so preoccupied with his explorations that he didn't pay much attention to sex life and you drifted apart physically. You're sorry things had to be that way, but that's the way they were. You do miss him tremendously and of course you're *terribly* sorry he was murdered. You certainly hope the police are able to find his murderer. You have hired detectives to help dig out clues for the police. And mind you get that straight, you haven't hired detectives to help the police solve the murder; that wouldn't be smart; you have only hired detectives to help unearth clues which will be turned over to the police so they can solve the crime.

"Now then, here's something I want you to do."

"What?"

I said, "Give me a sheet of paper."

She opened a drawer and tore a sheet of paper from a sketchbook.

I took my pen and wrote on it, "I hereby authorize and empower the firm of Cool & Lam to try to locate and take possession of the carved jade Buddhas which were stolen from my husband's collection in the penthouse."

I pushed the paper and the fountain pen over to her.

She read it and said, "Don't you want to put the date on there?"

I shook my head.

"Not even the date of the burglary?"

Again I shook my head.

"Why do you want this?"

"I may need it."

She hesitated a moment, then signed her name.

I took the paper, folded it, put it in my pocket and said, "Be seeing you, Phyllis."

She looked disappointed. "I wish you weren't always in such a hurry, Donald."

"So do I," I said, and walked out.

Chapter Sixteen

I drove around the block twice sizing up the place.

It was dark and I couldn't tell too much about it, but there was a light on in a front room, and the place seemed quiet and settled. Certainly there were no evidences of excited activity.

It was steeped in respectability with heavy vines growing all over the front porch. The place fairly radiated quiet dignity.

I parked the agency car, walked up the steps, and before I rang the bell I took the jade idol I had with me and hid it in the deep shadows of the vine. I didn't feel it would be a good idea to take that idol in there with me. If the guy was teamed up with Sylvia and she had stolen that idol for him, it was a cinch he'd know all about me and all about the idol by this time.

I pulled the vine over the idol and rang the bell.

The man who came to the door was even shorter than I was. He was somewhere around fifty and there was an air of watery-eyed apology about him that reminded me of an alley dog whose tail, tucked down between his legs, indicated that he expected to receive only kicks and stones as he went through life.

"I'm looking for Mortimer Jasper," I said.

"I am Mortimer Jasper," the man said, the watery blue eyes looking me over with mild curiosity.

"My name's Lam," I told him. "Donald Lam. I'm a private detective. Can I talk with you?"

"I don't see why not, Mr. Lam. Would you like to come in?"

I followed him into the house. We went through a small reception hall and into the front room where I had seen the light glowing in the window.

This room was fixed as a combination study, den and workshop.

There was a big desk, a little jeweler's bench with some tiny jeweler's lathes, a big safe with a double combination, a binocular microscope, some books, a big, heavy swivel chair back of the desk and two old-fashioned leather-bottomed chairs on the other side of the desk.

"Sit down," he told me in a quiet, gentle voice. "Tell me what I can do for you, Mr. Lam."

"I'm on rather a delicate mission."

"Is that unusual?"

"No."

"Perhaps you can tell me?"

I kept watching him, trying to find the best angle of approach. "Do you know a model named Sylvia Hadley?" I asked.

He picked up a pencil and started doodling on a pad of paper. He waited several seconds before he looked up and asked, "Does it make a difference?"

"It may make quite a difference."

"Perhaps you'd like to talk?"

I said, "I'm a professional, Mr. Jasper."

"A professional?"

"A detective."

"You told me."

"I get money for the work I do."

"Shouldn't you?"

"I came to tell you something that I think may make a difference."

"Tell me then."

"As I explained, Mr. Jasper, I'm a professional."

"As I said, tell me."

"You knew that Dean Crockett was dead."

"I read the papers."

"Dean Crockett had two very valuable carved jade Buddhas. I understand the jade was of beautiful color and texture and without flaws. The carving was exquisite. In the forehead of each Buddha was a blazing red ruby cunningly recessed, which gave the effect of a circle of animate fire within the brain of the Buddha."

"Interesting," he said, still doodling.

"The night before Crockett was murdered one of these jade idols was stolen. Three weeks before his death, another one had been stolen. Mr. Crockett considered them absolutely priceless."

The watery eyes looked up from the pad on which Jasper was doodling, then looked down again and followed the pencil as he made a series of interlacing triangles, put small circles on the points.

"I know who took the idols."

"Do you indeed?"

"Within a short time the police will know."

"How short a time?"

"Perhaps a few minutes."

"Go on."

"Sylvia Hadley," I said, "is an opportunist. She is a young woman who gets around. She is beautiful. She is clever. She is talented. She is uninhibited, and she has had very little experience with the police.

"When the police interrogate her, she will break down and tell them that from time to time she has, in addition to other things, stolen small but very choice articles of jewelry." I said nothing and Jasper said nothing. The pencil kept doodling along on the pad, making interlacing triangles and putting circles on the points.

"She will mention your name," I said at length.

"She has no reason to," he said, without looking up.

"The police," I said, "will make an investigation. They are probably securing a search warrant right now."

I quit talking and again there was silence, broken only by the whispering noise of the pencil sliding along the paper as it made its endless pattern of interlacing triangles.

"They will come here," I said. "There is not much time. Can I be of help to you?"

"In what way?"

"I represent the estate of Dean Crockett. I am working for his widow, Phyllis. I have been charged with recovering the stolen idol. There is a reward. If you facilitated the recovery of the stolen idol, you would receive three thousand dollars reward from the insurance company.

"The insurance company would, of course, want to be certain that it was not dealing with the thief or with any representative of the thief before they would pay the reward. That is where I fit into the picture.

"I could state that you had called me before the police had any lead to Sylvia Hadley. I could state that you told me you had this article of jewelry; that you had purchased it from a young woman who had said that it had been in her family for some years, having descended through her grandfather who was an old China trader; that it wasn't until you read of Dean Crockett's death and a description of the missing idol that you realized perhaps you had the mate to that idol and, therefore, you called me.

"That would take you off the hook as far as receiving stolen property is concerned, and you would get a three-thousand-dollar reward from the insurance company—perhaps more."

"And what do you want in return?"

This was where I had to make it good. If I made it too cheap, he'd get suspicious; if I made it too steep, he'd throw me out.

I waited until the watery eyes looked up into mine. "One thousand dollars," I said. "Cash."

"And if I shouldn't have one thousand dollars—cash?"

"I think you do have."

"Pardon me," he said. "The telephone."

He got up and walked past me out of the room, down the hall. I heard him pick up a telephone and say, "Hello, hello… yes." Then a door closed and I could hear only the rumble of his voice without making out anything that was said.

Evidently there were two phones in the house; one in the office and one which was on a separate line which rang in the back of the house.

I sat there for a while, thinking.

My ears are good but I hadn't heard any telephone ring. How did I know there were two separate lines?

I jumped up, moved over to the desk and picked up the telephone gently.

I was in time to hear Jasper's voice saying, "You take care of it, then," and the line clicked.

I dropped the telephone as though it had been hot and was back in my chair smoking a cigarette by the time Jasper came padding in through the door.

"My friend," he said, "you take a lot for granted."

"In my business, sometimes you have to."

"Perhaps too much."

"Perhaps."

"What assurance do I have that you would play fair?"

"In your presence, I would telephone Mrs. Crockett. I would tell her that I was telephoning from my apartment; that you had phoned me earlier in the afternoon; that I had gone to see you and that you had told me about having a Buddha which looked like the missing one of the pair; that you wanted her to come and view it, but that I hated to intrude upon her sorrow."

Again the pencil started doodling; this time putting circles on top of all of the triangular points and then putting diamonds on top of the circles.

Jasper looked at his watch.

I looked at mine.

"There is not much time," I said.

"There is enough," he remarked.

I waited for him to go on.

Abruptly he straightened. He said, "You will write as I dictate."

He handed me a pad of paper and a pen.

"I want to know what you're going to dictate first," I said.

He said, "You will write, 'I Donald Lam, a duly licensed private detective, received a telephone call from Mortimer Jasper at two o'clock this afternoon. Mr. Jasper told me that he thought he had one of the missing idols from the Crockett collection; that he had bought it in good faith and that he had read with very great surprise the description of the jade Buddhas which had been stolen from the Crockett collection.

"'I went to see Mortimer Jasper, and Jasper showed me the idol which he had. I told him that it was an exact duplicate of the idol that had been stolen, and Mr. Jasper turned it over to me, taking this written statement as a receipt and as evidence of his good faith. I am to return the idol to the owner.

"'Mr. Jasper told me that he had paid one thousand dollars for the idol and that he wanted to get his money back out of it, but, aside from that, he had no interest in any financial return of any sort.'"

I played it dumb. "I can get you three thousand dollars," I said.

"Certainly," he told me. "You will get me three thousand dollars and perhaps more. But in the meantime I will have this written statement of yours for my protection. In the event anything goes wrong, I will use this written statement. I will not use it unless it becomes necessary.

"You have come to me with a proposition that may be fishy. I don't know. You state that you are representing the estate. That much I do know because I read in the papers that your firm was called upon to guard the collection.

"Now, my friend, as you have remarked, time is short and we either do business or we don't."

"I'm not in this for my health," I said. "I get the thousand dollars."

"Of course."

"That must be in cash. This is a confidential transaction between the two of us."

"It is a confidential transaction," he said.

"But certainly," I assured him.

"Start writing then," he told me.

"You'll have to dictate it over," I said.

He dictated it over and I read it, hesitated, then signed it. He opened the upper right-hand drawer in his desk, took out the jade Buddha, took a wallet from his pocket, counted out ten one-hundred-dollar bills and handed me both the jade Buddha and the money.

I pocketed the money, took the jade Buddha, said, "There may not be much time. I want to get out ahead of the police."

"I want you to," he said.

He escorted me to the door. He didn't offer to shake hands and I didn't offer to shake hands.

I hurried across the sidewalk, jumped into the agency car, switched on the ignition and the headlights, jerked the lever of the transmission over into the driving position and was just starting from the curb when I felt the ominous, cold circle in the back of my neck.

"Take it easy, buddy," the voice said. "Drive around the corner to the right. Go two blocks. There's a vacant lot. Drive into that."

I did some fast thinking. "Who are you?" I asked.

"It doesn't make any difference."

"What do you want?"

"We'll tell you."

"Cops?" I asked.

"Don't ask questions. Just keep driving."

I kept on driving, turned the car into the vacant lot.

"Turn off the engine and the switch," the voice said.

I did so.

"Now the lights."

I snapped them off.

"Put your hands up over your head, clasp your fingers on the top of your head."

I did as directed.

Hands frisked me for a weapon.

"Get out."

I got out.

Two men got out. They were big men and it must have been hard for them to have crouched down out of sight in the back of the agency car while I was walking into their trap.

"A little squirt, aren't you?" one of the men said.

It was the other one who hit me as I turned; a blow to the side of the head that sent stars dancing in front of my eyes, and made me sick at my stomach. The other man swung a fist and caught me in the solar plexus.

I went down gasping for air. One of the men kicked me in the ribs. I made a lunge and wrapped my arms around his leg, caught him off balance and pulled him down.

I heard somebody laugh, then something hit me on the head and that was the last I knew.

Chapter Seventeen

It was nine-thirty when I recovered consciousness. I was lying there in the dark shadows of the vacant lot. There was no sign of the agency car.

I moved and it felt as though knives were stabbing me, but I got to my hands and knees and then unsteadily to my feet. I searched my pockets. The thousand dollars was gone, all of my own money was gone; my agency credentials remained, my wristwatch remained. My notebook, fountain pen and keys were still in my pocket. Aside from that, I had been cleaned of everything including the Buddha.

I tried walking. I made slow and painful progress, but I could move along and gradually the tortured muscles limbered up enough so I could take longer steps. But it hurt too much to straighten up, and I was partially doubled forward.

I thought I could make it to the light at the corner, but halfway there I began to get dizzy. I felt the sidewalk going round and round and grabbed hold of a mailbox as it came by. I clung to the mailbox and was sick.

After a while, headlights illuminated me, then I heard a car slide to a stop.

A voice called, "Hey, buddy, snap out of it."

I looked up and tried to grin.

"Come on over here. Let's have a talk."

It was a police car; a radio prowl. Two officers were in the front seat.

I walked across to it.

"What are you celebrating?" one of the men asked.

"I'm not celebrating," I said.

"Hell, that's blood on his shirt," the other one said. "Hey, what happened?"

"A couple of thugs took me in the vacant lot, rolled me and left me for dead."

"Got a driver's license?" one of the officers asked.

I put my hand in my pocket and pulled out my identification.

One of the officers studied the wallet with its cards of identification. The other kept his eyes on me.

The officer with the wallet gave a low whistle. "The guy's a private eye, Jim."

"Private eye, huh?"

"That's right."

"Name's Donald Lam."

The other one said to me, "What are you doing out here, Donald Lam?"

"I was calling on a man in connection with an investigation I was making. While I had my car parked in front of his house, two thugs got in the back of the car and crouched down in the shadows. I jumped in the car without looking and...well, they had me dead to rights. One of them stuck a gun in the back of my neck and told me to drive into a vacant lot down the street."

"Where's your car now?"

"Evidently they took it."

"You got the license number and all that?"

"That's right."

"All right. We'll put out a bulletin on it and maybe catch them—you look beat up pretty bad....Who were you calling on out here?"

"A man who lives around here."

"Let's have his name."

"It was confidential business."

"Who the hell you think you're kidding? Let's have his name."

"Mortimer Jasper," I said.

"Where does he live?"

"About a block and a half down and turn to the right."

"Get in," the officer said. "Show us."

I got in the car and directed them to Jasper's house.

"All right, Lam. Out you go," the officer said.

It was agony getting out, but one of the men helped me while the other one stayed with the prowl car to monitor the short-wave radio.

I went up the steps of the house, and the officer rang the bell. After a minute the door was opened.

Mortimer Jasper stood in the doorway, his manner apologetic, his watery blue eyes mildly curious. "Is there something?" he asked.

"I'm an officer," the man said. "This fellow claims he was calling on you earlier this evening on a matter of business. Two men jumped on him and rolled him."

"Calling on me?" Jasper asked, his voice rising at just the right note of incredulous surprise.

"That's right."

"But that is impossible. I have had no callers all evening."

"Take a look at him," the officer said, turning me around so the light from the doorway came on my features.

Jasper said, "I don't know what kind of a racket this is, but I have never seen the man before in my life."

The officer looked at me appraisingly. "Okay, Lam," he said, "we'll take you to headquarters. Perhaps you can think up a better story by the time you get there."

The officer walked me back to the car.

The officer in the car said, "How'd you come out?"

"Jasper says he never saw the guy in his life," the officer said.

"I've been busy checking on the radio," the officer behind the wheel said. "He's a private operator, all right, has a license and is in good standing. They're working on this Crockett case. You know, Dean Crockett who was murdered. Inspector Giddings and Sergeant Sellers are working on that. They want him brought in."

"Well, I've already told him we're going to take him in," the other officer said.

They nodded to me. "Make yourself comfortable, Lam. You're going to headquarters. They want to talk with you."

Chapter Eighteen

Inspector Giddings looked me over. "Well, well," he said, "you certainly look as though you'd been put through the meat grinder. Now, cut the comedy and tell me what *really* happened."

I tried to grin, but my face was too lopsided with swelling, and one eye was pretty well puffed up. It hurt when I straightened up. "I ran into a door in the dark going to the bathroom," I said.

Giddings gave me the benefit of a professional inspection; the way a trainer might look over a battered-up prize fighter in between rounds to see whether it was worthwhile throwing in the towel.

"You look as though you took the full count," he said.

"Only the count of nine," I told him.

"You think you're still in there fighting?"

"Yes."

He threw back his head and laughed at that. "Hell," he said, "you took the full count, Donald. You really did. You've been down and now you're out."

"I only heard nine," I said.

"Your ears were bad. I tell you, you're out."

"Meaning what?"

"Out. O-u-t. Do I have to spell it for you?"

"All right," I told him, "you're doing the talking."

"Now," he said, "you're beginning to get some sense. I'm doing the talking and it's damn near time that you recognized it. You know, we don't like to have smart private dicks playing around in murder cases.

"You can imagine how it would look to have the public pick up a newspaper and see that Donald Lam, a pint-sized private detective, had solved the Crockett murder case while the police were running around in circles."

Giddings paused and shook his head. "That would be what we call bad public relations.

"When you private eyes find out anything that has to do with a crime, you come right to us and tell us, and then we carry on from there."

"And do you tell me what's happening on my own tips?" I asked. "Or do I get to read it in the newspapers?"

He grinned in a fatherly way and said, "You get to read it in the newspapers, Donald. Now then, suppose we have an understanding and you start at the beginning and tell me just what this is all—"

The door pushed open, and Frank Sellers came hurrying in.

"Hi, Frank," Giddings said. "We've got a beat-up little canary here. I'm just telling him about the way we like to have canaries sing. We like to listen to them."

"Provided they sing the right tune," Sellers said.

"Exactly," Giddings agreed.

Sellers said, "Well, Pint Size, you've gone and done it again, eh?"

"I haven't done anything," I said.

"No, you don't look like it," Sellers admitted. "You've been more done against than doing."

He threw back his head and laughed.

Giddings grinned.

"I've just told this guy he's finished," Giddings said. "We're taking him out of the ring. He's had the full count."

"Well, what do you know, what do you know," Sellers said, rubbing his hands as though his knuckles started tingling at the spectacle of my bruised face and the thought of the beating I'd taken.

He turned to Giddings. "It's like I told you. The little bastard has a certain amount of brains and a hell of a lot of ingenuity. The trouble is he has nothing to back it up with. He's always leading with his chin, and somebody's always working him over. I'll bet I've seen that guy a dozen times when he looked as though he should have been in the hospital—all from sticking his neck out in some damn case where he should have gone to the police."

"Doesn't the bastard ever learn?" Giddings asked.

"Not so far," Sellers said.

Giddings' face was hard. "We'll learn him this time," he said grimly.

"I doubt it," Sellers said. "He has an affinity for sticking his face in front of fists. Don't you, Donald?"

I didn't say anything.

Giddings said, "I'm just going through the process of making a Christian out of the guy. I'm glad you got here, Frank." He turned to me. "Let's hear the *full* story, Lam."

"Yeah," Sellers said, pulling out a chair and sitting down. "The *full* story."

He pulled a cigar out of his pocket, twisted off the end with his teeth, spat the little gob of tobacco on the floor, lit the cigar and acted like a man preparing to enjoy a good show. "Go ahead, Pint Size, start talking and it had better be true."

"I don't have anything to talk about."

"Now, look," Giddings said, "we've got lots of ways of making people talk, and we don't have to do any brainwashing, either. We put pressure on you, Donald, my boy. We put the pressure on you right up and down the line. You can't make a living in this town if the police are against you, and if you're smart, you know that."

"He's smart," Sellers said. And then after a moment, added, "But tricky, awfully damn tricky."

"*You've* never lost anything tagging along with me," I told Sellers.

"Well, no," he admitted, puffing thoughtfully at his cigar. "I can't say I have, but I don't think that would have been true if I'd sat back and waited for you to deal the hand the way you wanted it. After you get the cards shuffled, I've taken the deck out of your hand and done the dealing myself."

"All right," I told him, "I'm still shuffling. When I'm ready for the deal, you can take the cards."

Giddings shook his head. "No, we don't like that, Donald. Maybe Sellers has confidence in you, but I haven't. I'm one skeptical sonofabitch. I don't trust *anybody*."

"You can say that again," Sellers said. "You can't stall around with Thad Giddings, Donald. You'd better start decorating the mahogany."

"Otherwise?" I asked.

Sellers made noises with his tongue against the roof of his mouth, the sort of rebuke that an indulgent mother gives to a small child.

"Begin at the beginning," Giddings said.

I said, "I don't have a thing in the world except suspicions. I hate to—"

"That's good enough for us," Giddings said.

"But I hate to make accusations just predicated on suspicion."

"We do it all the time, talking among ourselves," Sellers said. "Just don't say anything to anybody else, Donald—not the newspapers."

I said, "It all starts with a model who poses for artists and photographers in the nude."

"You're not referring to our little friend, Sylvia Hadley, the babe who was posing for Mrs. Crockett the afternoon her husband got bumped off, are you?"

"That's the one."

"What do you know!" Sellers said, and turned to Giddings. "That's one thing about Donald. He gets around with the babes. If there's a babe in the picture, she starts unloading on his shoulder, and Donald's really good at taking it from there. I guess they must want to mother the guy. He looks sort of helpless and unprotected. They feel they have to change his diapers. I've seen it happen a dozen times."

"Go on," Giddings said. "What about Sylvia Hadley?"

I said, "I think she's some kind of a fence."

"A fence? That babe?"

I nodded.

"He's nuts," Giddings said, turning to Sellers.

Sellers shook his head. "Let him go on, Thad. Let him ramble. He's got an angle in this somewhere, but we can figure it out if we let him talk. Go on, Donald. You think she's a fence. What makes you think so?"

I said, "She's been going with an older man, a man by the name of Mortimer Jasper, who's some kind of a collector and—well, it stands to reason, she wouldn't have any interest in him, that is, any real romantic interest—he's doing something for her."

"What?" Giddings asked.

"I think he's supplying her with…well, it's just a hunch, but I think he supplies her with information about the value of things, and I think Sylvia picks them up and then gets rid of them."

Giddings looked at Sellers and said, "For God's sake, how dumb can a guy get?"

"Shut up, Thad," Sellers said, his eyes boring into mine. "Go ahead, what's the pitch, Donald? You've got a reason for thinking this. What gives it to you?"

"That's what I'm trying to tell you," I said.

"Okay, go on. What happened?"

"Well," I said, "I tried to follow it up, that's all. I went out to call on Jasper and ask some discreet questions. I never even got in to see the guy. When I stopped the car and started to get out, a couple of goons came out and made me drive to a vacant lot. Then the guys beat the hell out of me."

"On that point we're willing to take your word for it," Giddings said, grinning. "That not only sounds logical, but there's evidence to support it."

"You think there was some connection between Jasper and these two goons?" Sellers asked.

"Hell no," I told him. "Get it straight. I think this jane, Sylvia Hadley, had these two strong-arm men follow me to see where I was going. When they saw I was getting hot on the trail, they worked me over. The idea was to keep me out of circulation for a while."

"Did they take anything?" Sellers asked.

"What do you mean, take anything?"

"You didn't have any evidence or anything they wanted?"

"If I'd had the evidence," I told him, "I'd have been playing it closer to my chest. I wouldn't have left myself wide open. Hell no, all I had was a hunch."

Sellers and Giddings exchanged glances. "The guy may have something," Sellers said, "with the cart before the horse, if you know what I mean, Thad."

"I get you," Thad said. "It's worth a try."

There was silence for a moment, then Giddings jerked his thumb at me. "What do we do with this guy?"

"Take him along," Sellers said.

Giddings shook his head.

"You don't know him like I do," Sellers said. "He may be playing a deep game. Take him along. Keep him with us all the time. In that way, if there's anything wrong with his story, the jane will let us see it as soon as we walk in with Pint Size here. She'll think he's double-crossed her and start squawking, and we can take it from there."

"I don't like taking him," Giddings said.

"If we don't take him, we're licked," Sellers said. "He'll hash things up for us."

"He wouldn't dare."

"The hell he wouldn't," Sellers said. "He's got more guts than any six guys you ever saw. That's the reason he's getting beat up all the time. He has no sense of discretion."

"We could lock him in a cell."

"He'd spring himself with a writ inside of fifteen minutes," Sellers said.

"Not if we left word that he couldn't get to a phone, and—"

"And then he'd sue us for a million dollars' damages and make it stick," Sellers said. "I've played around with this guy before. He's dynamite. He's fast on his feet. You do like I say, Thad. We take him along."

"Okay," Giddings said. "You're the boss. If that's what you say, that's what we do."

"Okay. On your feet," Giddings said to me.

I tried getting up out of the chair. The tortured muscles simply wouldn't respond. My legs didn't have enough strength to do the lifting.

Giddings grabbed me under the armpits, hoisted me to my feet. "Keep those muscles moving," he said, "otherwise they'll get sore as hell."

"What do you think they are now?" I asked him.

He just grinned. "Come on."

They got me to the elevator, down to a squad car and made time out through the traffic.

Inspector Giddings did stuff with the desk clerk at the apartment house. "We're going up to Sylvia Hadley's apartment," he said. "We want to ask her a couple of questions. Don't announce us."

"Very well," the clerk said.

"You heard me," Giddings said.

"I heard you."

"If we're announced, we'll take it as an unfriendly gesture," Giddings told him. "Come on."

We got in the elevator, went up to the hall and down the hall to Sylvia Hadley's apartment.

Frank Sellers banged on the door.

The door opened a couple of inches, held taut by a brass chain.

Sellers showed his badge and identification card all in a nice leather folder.

"Police," he said. "We want to talk with you."

"I've told you everything I know," Sylvia said.

"I know," Sellers said, "but we want to talk with you some more....Come on, open up. We haven't got all night to stand here and argue."

She opened the door.

The three of us trooped in.

She took a look at me and said, "Donald, what happened?"

"I ran into a door," I told her.

"And what are you doing here with these men?"

"They brought me along for the ride."

"We'll do the talking," Sellers said. "Donald was here earlier, wasn't he, Sylvia?"

"Yes."

"What did you tell him?"

"Nothing...that is, just some of the things I told you."

"What about Mortimer Jasper? What did you tell him about Jasper?"

From the look of sudden dismay on her face, Sellers knew he'd struck pay dirt.

"Go on. What did you tell him?"

"I didn't tell him a thing; not a damn thing!" Sylvia blazed. "And if he told you anything about Mortimer, he...he's lying, he's—"

"Take it easy, take it easy," Sellers said. "What about Mortimer Jasper?"

"Nothing about him."

"What's your connection with him?"

"I don't have any."

"You know him?"

"I...I've met him."

"And you didn't tell Donald Lam anything about him?"

"I did not!" she blazed. "I don't know what he told you, but whatever it was, it's a lie."

Sellers settled himself in a chair, crossed his ankles in front of him, pulled out another cigar. "What do you know, what do you know," he said in a tone of intense self-satisfaction. It was the voice of a man who has just been advised he's won the Irish Sweepstakes.

He bit off the end of a fresh cigar, spat it out on the worn threadbare carpet of the apartment, struck a match, held it to the cigar, puffed it a couple of times, said again, "What do you know?"

"I don't like cigars," Sylvia Hadley snapped.

Sellers might have had putty in his ears for all the attention he paid to that remark. He took a couple of deep, contented puffs, grinned across at Giddings and said, "We're in the money now."

Giddings raised his eyebrows at Sellers. Sellers nodded, turned to Sylvia and said, "You do know this Mortimer Jasper?"

"I tell you I've met him, yes."

"Been out with him?"

"I've been to dinner with him."

"Anything else?"

"That's all."

"Any passes?"

"He's old enough to be my father."

"They still make passes," Sellers said. "He could be old enough to be your great-grandfather and he'd still make passes. They might not find a receiver, but they're always trying a forward pass."

"Well...that isn't—Mortimer Jasper isn't like that."

"Didn't care about you as a dish?" Sellers asked.

"I tell you, of course not. He's a gentleman."

"Okay, then," Sellers said, grinning, "what *was* the pitch? What did he want? Why should he buy you a meal?"

"He...he likes me, I think. It was a fatherly interest."

"Oh, he took you out because he liked you, eh?"

"I guess that was it."

"But no passes?"

"No passes."

"Be your age," Sellers said.

Sylvia said nothing.

"What do you *know* about Mortimer Jasper?" Giddings asked.

"Very little," she said.

"How did you meet him?"

"I've forgotten. I think I was introduced to him at some gathering, probably something that Mr. Crockett put on."

"You went to the Crockett blowouts?"

"Sometimes."

"How did you happen to get in on those?"

"I was invited."

"By whom?"

"Mr. Crockett—or Mrs. Crockett."

"Sometimes Crockett invited you?"

"Yes."

"Another fatherly interest?"

"He…he liked to have people there who could liven things up a bit."

"And you livened things up a bit?"

"I tried to."

"And that's where you met Jasper?"

"It may have been. I don't know. I can't remember."

"You don't remember when you first met the guy?"

"No."

"How long ago?"

"I can't tell you that either."

"When was the time he took you out to dinner?"

"Which time?"

"Oh, was it more than once?"

"Yes."

"How many times?"

"I can't remember. Several."

"Well, well, well," Sellers said. "We're getting more and more chummy. Now, what does Mortimer Jasper do? What's his line?"

"He's retired."

"What does he have to occupy his mind? What keeps him from going to seed mentally?"

"I don't know."

"What did he talk about when he was with you?"

"I couldn't tell you that. We discussed various things."

"Sex?"

"I told you no."

"Making money?"

"I think he has plenty of that."

"Art?"

"Yes. He's interested in art."

"Jewelry?"

"Well, he's interested in precious stones, but not so much jewelry."

"Any particular branch of art?"

"No particular branch. He discussed the beautiful."

"He included you in that category?" Sellers asked.

"He didn't say so."

"But he looked you over?"

"How do I know what he was looking at?"

"My, but you're being cooperative," Sellers said. "You know, we *could* make things a little rough for you in this thing, Miss Hadley. Perhaps you'd better be a little more cooperative."

"About what?"

"About Mortimer Jasper, to begin with. You ever give him any money?" Sellers asked.

"No, of course not. Why should I give *him* money?"

"Okay," Sellers said. "Did he ever give you any money?"

She hesitated.

"Remember," Sellers said, "we have ways of finding these things out. We can get a subpoena on his bank account, and—"

"He gave me a check for a thousand dollars."

"Well, what do you know," Sellers said, rubbing his hands. "What do you know! We're beginning to get places!"

"No, you're not," she flared. "It was just a…a loan."

"For what?"

"I wanted some things. I wanted some clothes, and I wanted to get caught up on my car payments."

"What do you know," Sellers said.

"I wish you'd quit saying that over and over," she blazed. "Don't you know anything else? You're getting on my nerves."

Sellers grinned and said, "Now, look, Sylvia, you're getting a little angry. Don't do that. You wouldn't want to do anything that would forfeit my friendship, would you?"

"You can take your friendship and—"

"Tut-tut," Sellers interrupted. "You're going to need it, Sylvia."

"Why the hell should I want the friendship of any dumb cop?"

"In the first place, I'm not dumb. In the second place, you get along very well with your friends. Here's a guy that's old enough to be your father; you go out to dinner with him, you discuss art, you don't have anything particularly in common, he isn't interested in you as a woman but only as a dining companion who talks about art. You can't remember when it was you met him or how you met him—just sort of a casual acquaintance—and the guy digs up a thousand bucks. Now, you take a girl that has friends like that and she can go a long ways."

Sylvia turned toward me. "How does this guy fit into it?" she asked.

"Who?"

"Donald Lam here."

"Well, we just took him along to keep him out of circulation for a while," Sellers said. "You know, Donald gets into trouble if you let him run around loose."

She said, "If I thought Donald Lam was responsible for this, I'd...I'd tell a lot more things."

"Well, well," Sellers said, "what do you know. What other things, Sylvia?"

"I've said all I'm going to say."

"That's what you think," Sellers said. "What do you say, Thad?"

"I think we ought to check," Giddings said.

"So do I," Sellers said. "Get your things on, Sylvia. You're going places."

"Where?"

"Just a little ride."

"You can't take me to headquarters and question me any old time you want to. I've got a date."

"Ain't that too bad," Sellers said. "Another guy gets stood up—well, that's the way it goes. The best-looking guys always cop the prize. You're going for a ride."

Sylvia looked at me and said, "Somehow I have an idea you're tied up in this. If you are, I'm going to—"

She stopped, but continued to look at me.

"You're going to what?" Sellers asked.

"Nothing," she said.

"I think this is worth looking into a *lot* further," Giddings said to Sellers.

"So do I," Sellers said. "I think we're hitting pay dirt. Come on, Sylvia, get your things on."

She started for the bedroom.

Sellers got up and followed her.

"Give a girl some privacy," she blazed. "I don't want a man looking over my shoulder while I'm getting ready to go out."

"All you need is a coat," Sellers told her, "and I'll help you on with it."

"How do you know what I need?"

"I can tell by looking at you," Sellers told her.

He helped her on with a coat. She adjusted a hat in front of a mirror.

"Come on," Sellers said.

We went down in the elevator and got in the squad car. After a few blocks, Sylvia said, "This isn't the way to headquarters."

"Who said anything about headquarters?" Giddings asked.

"You mean you aren't— You don't have any right to take me anywhere except to headquarters."

"We're going to call on your friend, Mortimer Jasper," Sellers told her. "We want to check into that thousand dollars he gave you."

"Yes," Giddings said. "We're investigating another crime now."

"What crime?"

"Contributing to the delinquency of a minor," Sellers said.

"Aren't you funny!" she snapped. "I'm twenty-four years old and I was delinquent for ten years before I ever saw Mortimer Jasper."

"They always try to talk you out of it," Giddings said. "You take these kids fourteen and fifteen that are trying to buy drinks, and darned if they won't have some kind of a fake birth certificate, or license or something, always claiming they're old enough to do as they please and that nobody has a right to tell them what to do and what not to do."

"That's a funny thing," Sellers said. "Now, you take this babe. She may be nineteen or twenty, perhaps, but—"

"Oh, I'd put her under eighteen," Giddings said. "I would for a fact."

"Well, she talks older," Sellers said.

"Sure, she does. That's because of the very thing we're investigating. Men take advantage of them and it makes them hard and—"

Sylvia said, "I could spit on both of you guys."

Sellers laughed and said, "That's what comes of trying to tell a woman her age, Thad. Now, you wait another ten years and if you take four or five years off her age she'll beam and grin all over her face. But when a kid's a minor she wants to act grown-up."

Sylvia said something under her breath.

Sellers said, "I didn't hear that so well, Sylvia, but I hope it wasn't what I thought I heard. That's a naughty word." Sylvia sat in tight-lipped silence.

The officers drove the car for another five minutes, then eased it to a stop in front of Mortimer Jasper's house.

"What's the plan? We all go in?" Giddings asked.

"We all go in," Sellers said.

We got out of the car, moved slowly in a compact group up the cement walk.

Sellers rang the bell.

After a minute Mortimer Jasper opened the door.

"Officers," Sellers said. "We want to talk with you, and—"

Jasper looked past him to me and said, "How long is this going to keep up? This is the second time this lying sonofabitch has been out here with officers. I've never seen him before in my life."

"Never?" Sellers asked.

"Never in my life."

"Not even when the officers brought me out the first time?" I asked.

"You smart-aleck shyster, you crook, you bloodsucker, you—" Jasper caught himself.

"You seem to know a lot about him for a guy you've never seen before," Sellers said. "Take a look at this young lady. Do you know her?"

Giddings pushed Sylvia Hadley forward. She had been hanging back in the background.

"I tell you," Sylvia said, "I only—"

Giddings put his arm around her neck, clapped his hand over her mouth, said, "Shut up. This is Jasper's party. Let him do the talking."

"I...I think it's Miss Hadley," Jasper said, blinking his eyes. "I can't see so good out here. It looks like—"

"That's fine," Sellers said. "We'll come in, where the light's better."

Sellers pushed his way in. Inspector Giddings was keeping a tight hold on Sylvia Hadley.

I started to go in the door, then stumbled, fell to one knee, tried to catch myself, sprawled flat on the cement and lay there groaning.

"Come on, come on," Sellers said over his shoulder. "Get going, Donald."

I got to one knee, crawled to the edge of the porch and started retching.

Jasper said, "I demand to know the meaning of this."

"Come on," Sellers shouted angrily, "get the lead out of your pants, Donald. Every minute you give this guy he's thinking."

"I can't help it. I'm sick," I said.

"It's a stall," Giddings said. "He's trying to give the guy time to think."

"And why should I be needing time to think, please?" Jasper asked.

Sellers pushed Jasper on into the house, said, "Come on, Giddings. Bring Sylvia in, then you can go back and drag Lam in."

As they went through the door, I groped for and found the jade idol I had concealed in the vine, slipped it in my pocket and started crawling on hands and knees toward the door.

Giddings came out, grabbed me under the arm, jerked me erect and planted a knee in the small of my back. "Get going, you little bastard," he said. "This is a crucial time and you have to pull a stunt like this."

"I can't help it," I moaned.

"Get the hell in there."

"I'm being sick."

"Get sick on the guy's rug, for all we care," he said. "Get in."

Jasper was trying to spar for time. Sellers didn't intend to give him any time.

"All right, Jasper," Sellers said, "what's the pitch with you and Sylvia Hadley here?"

Sylvia said, "I told them, Mortimer, that—"

Again Giddings lunged toward her and clapped his hand over her mouth.

"We're doing the talking," Sellers said to Sylvia. "One more crack out of you and you'll spend the night in the detention ward. Now, Jasper, start doing some talking. Don't sit there trying to think up a good story because we're not going to give you that much time. Tell us the truth and start now."

Jasper said, "I know this young lady, but that is all. I've met her, and—"

"And why did you give her a thousand bucks if you scarcely knew her?" Sellers asked.

Jasper blinked his eyes, "Who said I gave her a thousand bucks?" he asked belligerently.

Sellers pushed toward him, stuck his face within six inches of Jasper's face and said, "*I* say you gave her a thousand dollars!"

Jasper tried to glance at Sylvia for a signal, but Sellers kept his face in the way. "Come on," he said, "start talking, start talking."

"She had a friend who wanted the thousand dollars," Jasper said. "This friend wanted to sell me an article of jewelry which I thought I could sell for a profit—I knew I couldn't go wrong at the thousand-dollar price. Sylvia was the intermediary. She said she was representing this friend, and I advanced her the thousand dollars but told her not to pay over a dime of the money until she had the merchandise in her hand."

"Did she get it?"

"I don't think so. I haven't heard. She is the one to tell you that."

"What was it?" Sellers asked.

"A jade idol, carved jade. As she described it, it was a very exquisite and…beautiful piece of Chinese workmanship. She said she could get it for a thousand dollars. Her friend was willing to sell it because she had to have some cash money."

"Did she say who her friend was?"

"No."

"Say it was Phyllis Crockett?"

"She didn't say, and I didn't ask."

"Are you familiar with the two jade Buddha pieces Dean Crockett had?"

"No."

"Do you think this could have been one of them?"

"I'm sure I couldn't say, because I haven't seen anything yet. It could have been. She told me her friend said that it had been in the family for a long time. The friend wanted to dispose of it. She said this friend needed some money very badly; that she had to have a thousand dollars, and Sylvia thought she could get it for a thousand dollars."

"Hell, you're going over and over the same story time after time trying to think," Sellers said. "Get your needle out of the same groove and go on to the rest of it. Did Sylvia turn over the money to this friend?"

"Not unless she got the merchandise. Unless, of course, she violated instructions or unless I was taken. After all, I know very little about Miss Sylvia Hadley. If she is in love, she might feel she would be willing to sacrifice Mortimer Jasper for her boyfriend. Women in love will do anything."

"How long ago did you give her this thousand bucks? Remember now, we're going to take a look at your books and trace the payment."

"It must have been…three or four weeks ago."

They were studying Jasper's face with the hard skeptical eyes of law enforcement officers. No one was paying any attention to anything other than his face, his voice, his watery meek eyes.

I slipped around behind the desk. There was an embossed leather wastebasket half full of papers. I eased the jade idol out of my pocket and dropped it in among the papers.

"You just gave her the thousand bucks on the strength of her say-so?" Sellers asked.

"That's right. I relied on her honesty."

"How long had you known her before you gave her this thousand bucks?"

"Not very long. I tell you I really know very little about her."

"How did she happen to come to you with this story?"

"I met her."

"Where did you meet her?"

He tried to look to Sylvia for a signal. Sellers grabbed him by the shoulders and spun him around.

"She came to me," Jasper said. "She had heard I was interested in certain objects of art. She wanted to know if it would be worth a thousand dollars to me to get a very old, very beautiful piece of jade...."

"That was the first time you met her?"

"That was the first time."

"And you told her it would be worth it to you?"

"Yes."

"And gave her the thousand dollars?"

"Yes."

"Without any more description of the jade piece than that— you gave a girl you had never seen before a thousand bucks.... Come on, Jasper, you're going to have to do better than that. We know you've been out with her. You've had her out to dinner—"

"That was after the thousand dollars."

"Not before?" Sellers asked. "Think carefully now, because you're going to find yourself in one hell of a jam in a minute."

"I can't think. I'm rattled," Jasper said. "I—"

"Before the thousand bucks?" Sellers asked.

"Yes," Jasper said.

"That's better. Now tell us the true story."

"I knew she was an artists' model," Jasper said. "I saw a painting of her. I wanted to know the model's name. I got her name and address and…well, I looked her up. I— Okay, what the hell. I was on the make."

"On the make, eh?" Sellers asked. "Did you get anywhere?"

"That's an embarrassing question," Jasper said.

Sylvia's half-scream sounded as though it was an epithet she was mouthing, but Giddings' hand over her mouth kept the sound from being articulate. It was only an animal squeal of rage.

"I gave her a thousand dollars," Jasper said.

"For a piece of jade?"

"For the friend who wanted to sell me the jade idol. She promised she would deliver it to me. I trusted her by that time. I had used the thousand-dollar deal to become friendly."

"How friendly?"

"Very friendly. I gathered that went with the deal as a part of it."

Sellers nodded to Giddings. Giddings took his hand down from Sylvia's mouth.

"You lying sonofabitch!" Sylvia screamed at him. "I've been around, but I wouldn't let you touch me with a ten-foot pole. You commissioned me to get those jade idols from the Crockett collection and promised me a thousand bucks apiece. You didn't give me the thousand dollars until I gave you the first idol. I'd have got both of them at one time, but Dean Crockett had one of them locked up when I grabbed the first one."

"Now, that's better," Giddings said, seating himself. "Sit down, folks, let's be comfortable."

"What do you know!" Sellers said, grinning.

"That is a complete fabrication," Jasper said with dignity. "In view of the accusation, I am going to insist that I be permitted to get in touch with my lawyer."

"Any objection to our looking around?" Sellers asked.

"For what?"

"To see if you've got a jade idol of that sort kicking around here."

"I can assure you I don't have anything of the sort."

"How about that safe?"

"There's a time lock on it. It can't be opened until nine o'clock tomorrow morning. That is for my protection in case of burglars. That is all."

"Any objection to our coming back in the morning to see what's inside?"

"I…I can assure you there is no such jade idol in there."

"How about the rest of the place?" Sellers asked.

"I have no objection to you looking around," Jasper said. "I can assure you, however, that this charge is entirely without foundation and any search would be completely fruitless." Sellers moved over toward the desk.

"I have nothing to conceal," Jasper said, "but I feel that this is unwarranted—this entire procedure."

"We're getting somewhere," Sellers said to Giddings. "Open up the desk. Let's take a look."

"If that desk is opened, *you're* going to open it," Jasper said, "and I don't think you have a search warrant."

"I'll damn soon get one," Sellers told him. "On the strength of what you've said I can get it."

"No, you can't," Jasper said.

Sellers looked at Giddings and frowned.

Giddings looked at Sylvia.

Abruptly Sylvia caught some signal from Jasper and clamped her lips shut in a firm, determined line of silence.

"Now, wait a minute," Sellers said. "Let's do some thinking. Little Pint Size was here earlier in the evening, and he got beaten up....He was looking for something...he was on the wrong track. He had the cart before the horse. He thought Sylvia was the— Now, wait a minute. Did he? Hell, he's not *that* dumb. He's...he's been bird dogging something."

"And he got beaten up," Giddings said.

"No doubt about that," Sellers told him. "The evidence is there all right."

"I know nothing about it. I had nothing to do with it. I have never seen this man before," Jasper said.

"But the officers came here with Lam?" Sellers asked.

"That's right."

"And you told them you'd never seen him before?"

"Right."

"So," Sellers said to Giddings, "he knew that he was getting involved in things. He's had an hour or two to clean things up. We probably aren't going to find anything incriminating in the whole joint."

"I can assure you, you won't," Jasper said. "But not because I have cleaned things up, as you term it."

Sellers walked over the office looking around.

Jasper, now sure of his ground, said, "Not without a search warrant, Officer."

"I can phone up and get a search warrant and we can wait right here and see you don't touch anything," Sellers said.

Jasper grinned. "Do that. On the information that you have so far, try getting a search warrant."

Sellers kicked the wastebasket out into the open. "Looks as though you'd been cleaning out a lot of files after you knew that you were in trouble," he said.

He looked down at the torn envelopes, the crumpled letters, and then suddenly something caught his eye. He shot his hand down into the wastebasket, felt around for a minute, then came up with the jade idol. "Well, well, well," he said. "What do you know! What do you know!"

Jasper stared at the jade idol as though he had been seeing things.

"Framed!" he screamed. "Framed! You planted that. That's a plant! That's a frame! That—"

His voice trailed away into silence.

"What do you know," Sellers said. "So it's a plant, is it? You can tell it to the judge—I'll bet you money this is the missing idol from the Crockett collection."

Sylvia was on her feet. "You double-crossing sonofabitch!" she shrieked. "You told me you'd taken care of that. You told me over the phone that you had all the evidence removed and—"

"Shut up!" Jasper shouted, with such concentrated venom in his voice that Sylvia caught herself in mid-sentence.

"It's all right," Sellers said, beaming at the two of them. "We don't need your story anymore. We've got all we need on both of you right now."

Sellers picked up the phone, dialed headquarters, said, "This is Frank Sellers. I'm out at the residence of Mortimer Jasper, 6286 Carrolton Drive....I think the guy is a fence.... We've discovered a jade idol in his wastebasket. It's green jade with a big ruby set deep in the forehead. I think it's the missing Crockett idol.

"Giddings is here with me. I want a radio car sent out to sew the place up. I'm coming into headquarters with Sylvia Hadley and a private detective named Lam. I'm going to make an affidavit and get a search warrant as soon as we get that idol identified. I want Mrs. Crockett alerted so that we can have her identify the idol....You got that? All right, have everything in readiness. I want this place sewed up tight until I get back with a search warrant. I think we're solving the Crockett murder along with the theft."

Sellers turned to Giddings and said, "You go call a prowl car, Thad. Tell them to keep an eye on this guy. Tell them to get here fast, to handcuff him and arrest him if they have to, for having stolen property in his possession, but I'd prefer to wait until we've had a positive identification. However, tell the radio officers to ride herd on him and not to let him out of their sight."

Jasper's face was a sickly green. "The Crockett murder," he said. "Oh, my God!"

Sellers turned to Sylvia. "You're coming with me, sister." He jerked his thumb at me and said, "You, too, Lam. Let's get started. Thad will have a squad car here within two minutes."

Chapter Nineteen

As we reached the sidewalk after the radio prowl officers had taken charge of Jasper, I said to Sellers in a low voice, "I suppose you'll want me along to help you when you question Sylvia Hadley?"

"To help me what?" Sellers asked.

"Question Sylvia Hadley," I whispered.

He threw back his head and laughed. "Listen, Pint Size, don't get exaggerated ideas. Your partner, Bertha Cool, claims you're a brainy little bastard. It's highly questionable, but don't let your publicity go to your head."

"You mean you don't want me anymore?"

"I don't want any part of you. Get lost. Go home and— I'll tell you what you do."

"Yes?" I said.

"Yes," he said. "I'll tell you *exactly* what to do. Do you know where there's an all-night drugstore?"

"Sure. But lots of them are open now."

"All right," he said. "Go to a drugstore and get two bits' worth of powdered alum."

"Two bits' worth of powdered alum is a lot of alum," I said. "Then what do I do?"

"Then go home, draw some water in the washbasin and put in the whole two bits worth of powdered alum."

"Then what?" I asked.

"Then," he said, "soak your head in it until it gets down to normal."

With that, Frank Sellers walked over to Sylvia and Giddings.

He was in great good humor. "All right, sister," he said to Sylvia, "we're on our way."

They climbed in the squad car. Giddings took the wheel. Sellers slammed the door. "Get lost, Pint Size," he said.

I had seen a service station three blocks down the street. I walked down to it. It was pretty painful going. I got the service-station attendant to stake me some dimes on the agency's credit card, and called Bertha.

"Where the hell are you?" Bertha demanded.

"I'm at a service station in the 5800 block on Carrolton Drive."

"What the hell are you doing out there?"

"I'm in trouble."

"You're always in trouble. What is it this time?"

"A couple of goons stole the agency car."

"What do you mean, they stole the agency car?"

"Just what I said."

"What would anybody want with that car?"

"They didn't want the car," I said. "They wanted to put me afoot. I need an automobile. I've got to have transportation. I've been beaten up pretty bad."

"Again?"

"Again."

"Where did you say you were?"

"At 58th and Carrolton Drive."

"All right," Bertha said. "I'll get out there."

"I've been bloodied up a bit," I said. "I keep a suitcase packed at the office. If you could pick up that suitcase, I'd have a clean shirt and I could change."

"All right," Bertha groaned. "I'll do it. My God, if there's anything in the theory of reincarnation, you must have been a football in your past life."

"Or a punching bag," I said, and hung up.

I called Phyllis Crockett. "Officers are going to see you to ask you to identify a jade Buddha as the missing statue that was taken the other night. Identify it, but don't do any more talking than you have to. Tell them you're waiting for me, that I've phoned I'm on my way up there. Be sure to tell them that.

"After they leave, don't go outside under any consideration. Stay there and wait for me—no matter how late it gets, wait there."

I didn't wait to give her a chance to ask questions or argue but hung up the phone.

It was half an hour before Bertha got there.

She said, "My God, you're a mess."

"That's what I told you. You brought the suitcase?"

"Yes."

"Got any money?"

"What the hell do you mean, have I got any money?"

I said, "Mine's gone."

"Now look," Bertha said, "you've got a right to carry a gun. Your license gives you the right to do that. Why don't you get so you can protect yourself instead of letting everybody beat you up?"

"Guns," I said, "cost sixty to seventy-five dollars—a good kind of a gun that I'd want to carry."

"Well, why don't you get one? But don't try to charge it as an expense. It'll be for your personal protection, and you take it out of your personal dividend."

I said, "Then every time they beat me up they'd take the gun away, and I'd go broke buying guns."

"You would, at that," Bertha agreed, without any sympathy. "Now you want a car. How the hell am I going to get back to *my* apartment?"

"There's a phone," I said. "Call a taxi while I'm changing my clothes."

"Call a taxi! Why you— What do you think I am?"

"Call a taxi," I said, "and charge it on an expense account to Mrs. Crockett. If you want I'll phone for the cab and pay for it, but I want some money."

Bertha took out her purse grudgingly, counted out five dollars and said, "That's going to last you until tomorrow morning… the idea of having me run around at night, playing chauffeur for you. What happened to the agency car?"

"About tomorrow morning," I said, "you'll hear from the police department, maybe sooner. They'll ask what's the idea of leaving the agency car parked in front of a fireplug."

"You think they'll park it in front of a fireplug?" she asked.

"Absolutely."

"You do the damnedest things," Bertha groaned, and squeezed herself into the telephone booth to phone for a taxi.

I took the suitcase to the washroom, changed my clothes, sponged off some of the dried blood on my face, and surveyed the swollen wreckage in the wavy mirror.

By the time I came out Bertha had left in the cab.

The service-station attendant seemed quite considerate. "You must have been in an accident," he said.

"That's right."

"What happened to your car?"

"Smashed all to hell," I told him.

I checked the gas on the car Bertha had brought out. It was half full.

I drove back down Carrolton Drive and took a look at Jasper's house as I went by. There was a police car in front of the place. They were still sitting on Jasper waiting until Sellers could get back with a search warrant.

I drove down about half a block and parked the car.

Putting two and two together, I knew that while I had been talking with Jasper he had only pretended to hear the phone ring in the other part of the house. What had actually happened, he'd gone to the phone and called his goons, told them to come and take care of me.

In order to do that, the men he called had to be close by. There wasn't time for them to have come from any distance. I felt pretty certain these men would be abreast of developments and would be keeping an eye on the place, so I checked the license number of every automobile that went past on Carrolton Drive.

A car came by that slowed down as it went past Jasper's house.

I got my car into motion and caught up with the other car about four blocks down the street. It was a late model sedan, license number NFE 799. Two fellows were in the front seat. They were big guys and I felt pretty certain the man at the wheel was the ape who had kicked at my ribs when I had grabbed his foot and pulled him down to the ground.

They turned to the right on 54th Street. I kept right on going to 53rd, then made a U-turn, beat it back to the place where I'd been, and waited.

In about five minutes the same car drove past again. Once more I followed the car. This time they drove down to the service station and stopped. The big man got out from behind the wheel and went into the phone booth.

I parked half a block down the street.

In about two minutes the big man dashed out of the phone booth, jumped in the car and they went away from there fast. I tagged along behind, taking a chance, keeping as close as I dared.

They made three right turns around the block, got back to Carrolton Drive, turned left, and went to 61st Street. They turned right on 61st, then turned left into a driveway.

I marked the place, and went on down 61st for two blocks, made a U-turn and came back.

Their car was in the driveway. The men were at the front door of a little bungalow. A moment later they entered and lights came on in the bungalow.

I parked my car and hurried over to the sedan in the driveway.

I put on gloves and tried the door. It was unlocked.

I looked inside, using a fountain-pen flashlight.

The car was registered to Lyle Ferguson, 9611 61st Street.

I opened the glove compartment and there was a pint flask of whiskey in there about two-thirds empty.

I picked up the flask by the neck with my gloved hand, closed the glove compartment, gently closed the door of the automobile, went back to Bertha's car, poured all the whiskey out into the gutter and carefully put the empty flask down on the floor boards. I tied a cord around the neck of the flask so I could hold it without smudging any prints that might be on it and drove to my apartment house.

Holding the empty whiskey bottle by the cord, I let myself into the apartment and proceeded to take the joint to pieces. I pulled out drawers, dumped things on the floor, pulled things out of the medicine cabinet, pulled suits off the hangers and turned the pockets wrongside out, pulled the bedding off the bed and upended the mattress. When I had wrecked the place, I went out and drove to a drugstore near the Crockett apartment house.

I phoned Phyllis Crockett. "Have the passage to the elevator fixed so I can come up," I said. "I'm going to sneak past the clerk to the elevators. Be sure I can get up to your place without any delay. Leave everything open for me."

I went to the apartment house and waited until a party came in that looked like they lived in the place. As they went through the door, I timed things so that I entered just behind them. One of the men saw me and held the door open for me.

I thanked him, took out a cigarette, asked him for a light and walked to the elevators with him. I kept him between me and the night clerk.

His party got off at the fifteenth floor. I went to the twentieth.

The door of the anteroom was opened.

I pressed the concealed button which brought the elevator down from the penthouse. I got in and went up.

Phyllis met me.

"Anybody here with you?" I asked.

"I'm all alone," she said. "Good heavens, Donald! What's happened to you?"

"I've been in an accident."

"What sort of an accident?"

"Some people," I said, "thought I was a punching bag. It took me quite a while to persuade them that I wasn't."

"Donald, you should see a doctor."

"A doctor should see me," I said, and tried to grin, but my face was swollen so badly that I knew it was a pretty lopsided attempt.

"What time is it?" I asked.

She looked at her wristwatch. "Twelve minutes past midnight."

I shook my head.

"What do you mean?"

"Twenty minutes past eleven," I said.

"Donald, what do you mean?"

I said, "Your watch is off. It's twenty minutes past eleven."

"Donald, it can't be. I've been watching television and...I know my watch is right."

"I got here at twenty minutes after eleven," I said.

She studied me for a moment, then grinned and said, "All right. Now tell me what happened to your face?"

"I think we're getting places," I said.

"In what way?"

"I think the police are going to clear up the case."

"The police?"

"Always the police," I said. "Never do anything that would keep the police from being the ones who get the credit. That's axiomatic in my business....Nobody has been calling for me?"

She shook her head.

"Bertha Cool, my partner, didn't call and want me?"

"No."

I said, "Well, I guess we're—" The telephone rang.

I nodded to Phyllis.

"If anybody wants to know if you're here, what do I tell them?" she asked.

"Tell them I'm here."

She answered the telephone, then turned to me. "It's your partner, Mrs. Cool. She wants you right away. She says its urgent."

I went over to the telephone. Bertha said, "Frank Sellers wants you right away, Donald."

"Where is he?"

"Headquarters. He says you're to call him at once, that I'm to get in touch with you and have you report at once."

I said, "Okay, Bertha. I'll get it."

Bertha said, "I hope you know what you're doing, Donald. Frank seems pretty well worked up about something."

"He's always worked up about something," I told her. "I'll call him."

I hung up the telephone, nodded to Phyllis, said, "This is the police now," and dialed headquarters.

I asked for Homicide Department and got Frank Sellers on the line.

Sellers said, "Where the hell are you, Donald?"

"Up in the Crockett apartment conferring with my client."

"How long you been there?"

"A little over an hour, I guess. Why?"

"I want you."

"You've had me," I said. "You told me to get lost. I'm lost."

"Now I'm going to find you again."

"I'm up here," I said.

"All right. I'm coming up," Sellers said, "and tell that Crockett dame to fix it so I can get up in that elevator without a lot of red tape rigmarole, otherwise I'll tear the place to pieces....I think you've been pulling a fast one, Pint Size, and if you have, I'm personally going to take *you* to pieces so you'll learn a lesson you'll *never* forget."

I said indignantly, "You wouldn't dare to make a threat like that if a couple of goons hadn't already softened me up."

It sounded as though Sellers was strangling on the telephone. I hung up.

Phyllis Crockett, who had heard the conversation, was watching me anxiously. "What is it, Donald?" she asked. "Are you in bad with the police?"

"I'm always in bad with the police," I told her. "It's chronic. It's constitutional. Frank Sellers is on his way up here. He may have somebody with him. He wants to come up without any trouble. Better telephone the desk and tell them to pass him on through and send somebody up with him so there won't be any trouble with the elevator."

"Donald, do I have to see the police at all hours of the night this way?"

"You do tonight," I told her.

"Donald, I'm going to put some hot witch hazel compresses on your face. I don't care who's coming up."

"Go ahead," I told her. "It's a good idea. Spread a lot of towels around as though you'd been working on my face for about an hour, and if you get an opportunity, be a little bit indignant with Frank Sellers that the police can't give a citizen better protection than I've been receiving."

"Won't that make him angry?" she asked.

"Sure," I said. "It'll make him sore as hell—at you. The more different things we can make him mad about, the less he can concentrate on any one of them."

"He's mad at something now?"

"Mad at something is right," I said. "He's really mad at me this time."

Chapter Twenty

The police got there right on schedule. They were mad, plenty mad, and scared.

"Well, well, well," Giddings said as they walked in, "a nice scene of domesticity—do your clients always furnish you with first-aid services, Lam?"

"This is an unexpected luxury," I said.

"All right, never mind the compresses and the repartee. Get up here. We want to talk with you."

Phyllis bent over me and removed the hot compress with the witch hazel pad underneath. I sat up on the davenport.

"Now, look, Donald," Frank Sellers said, "I'm friendly with your outfit. You're a tricky little bastard, but I've been telling Thad Giddings here that you won't double-cross a guy if he plays ball with you."

"Who's double-crossed whom?" I asked.

Giddings said, "Sylvia Hadley has talked."

"That's fine," I said. "I thought she would."

"Now then, the thing was just a hundred percent different from the way you told us you had it doped out, and by God, you knew it was. Mortimer Jasper wanted those two idols. She got one of them, and he paid her a thousand bucks. She was to get the other one. He was to give her a grand for that."

"Well, for Heaven's sake," I said, with the best air of innocence I could assume. "You mean that in place of Sylvia being the mastermind, it was Mortimer Jasper, and Sylvia was just a tool?"

"That's right," Sellers said patiently. "Now then, we're coming to something very, very interesting."

"What?" I asked.

"Jasper is raising hell. He says that *you* planted that idol in his wastebasket; that you had it stashed away out there on the porch someplace, and that when you came in, while we were all milling around, you managed to get over by the wastebasket and dropped it.

"Now, come to think of it, I do remember you standing around over that wastebasket, and it seems to me that I remember hearing some kind of a rustle in the papers as though some object had been dropped into the papers in the wastebasket.

"Jasper says that you recovered the idol that was stolen the other night, and that you switched that and made it appear that was the idol stolen three weeks ago, and that then you framed the whole thing on him. He's getting a lawyer and threatening suit against us for false arrest, malicious persecution, frame-up, and all the rest of it.

"The sonofabitch turns out to have a hell of a lot of political pull, and his lawyers work fast. Thad and I have been summoned to the chief's office at nine in the morning. It looks like hell."

I said, "Well, of course, Jasper has to blame the thing on someone—it's very fortunate for you gentlemen that you had me along, otherwise he'd have claimed you were the ones who framed him."

"Well, there's one answer to it," Sellers said, "and only one answer. Sylvia Hadley says that you recovered the idol she had concealed in Lionel Palmer's camera."

I didn't say anything for a minute, and they both stood staring at me in accusing silence.

"Now then," Sellers went on, "we want that idol and we want it *right now*, Donald. Then we've got an answer to Mortimer Jasper. Then we can go ahead and get this case buttoned up.

Otherwise he can claim you played us for suckers and we're out on a limb."

"And if it turns out you've been doing skulduggery," Giddings interposed, "I'm personally going to fix you so that all the compresses in the world will never get your face back into shape—and that's a promise!"

I sighed. "I don't know why you take the word of some crook on a deal like that. I suppose if I hadn't been along and Jasper had accused Giddings of planting that idol, you'd have stuck up for him, Sellers. But because he accuses me, you come running up here in the middle of the night....Okay, let's go get the idol."

"Where is it?"

"In my apartment."

"Let's go," Sellers said.

"I can get it first thing in the morning, and—"

"I said let's go," Sellers told me.

I got up and buttoned my shirt collar. "He said let's go," I said to Phyllis.

"I heard him, Donald," she said. "Do you feel all right to go?"

"Oh, sure," I said. "I'm in fine shape now."

"You're going to have a black eye," she said.

"That's nothing," I told her. "I'm always getting black eyes— the thing that's bothering me at the moment is I think I've got a broken rib. I probably should be taped up."

"You let me get a doctor for you, Donald, and—"

"Come on, let's go," Sellers said. "Donald is going to give us that idol."

"Well, now, wait a minute," I said. "I didn't say I was going to give it to *you*. That idol is technically the property of Mrs. Crockett, and—"

"That idol is evidence, and you know it," Sellers interrupted. "You had no business hanging on to it."

"But," I said, "it's not stolen property."

"What do you mean?"

I said, "Sylvia told me that Dean Crockett wanted her to take that."

"Yeah," Giddings said. "She tried to hand us that line—that lasted for just about two minutes."

"Well, she told me that and I believed her."

"The hell you did," Giddings said. "She made a deal with you. You were to believe her on that, and she wasn't going to blab about this other evidence that—" He broke off.

Sellers said, "Let's not do any more talking, Thad. Let's go get that idol."

Giddings glared at me, then said, "Okay, let's go over to the guy's apartment and get the idol. If it isn't in our hands within ten minutes, we'll work this guy over right."

The three of us went down in the elevator. Phyllis Crockett was watching me apprehensively.

"I'm coming back," I told her. "Don't go to bed, and fix it so I can come up."

She came toward me. "Here's a key to the anteroom, Donald."

"If he doesn't produce that idol, he's going to spend the night in a hospital," Giddings said.

"Come on, Pint Size," Sellers remarked impatiently, grabbing my coat collar and hustling me into the elevator.

We went down and transferred to the apartment house elevator at the twentieth floor. The squad car was waiting outside.

The two officers didn't say a word as they drove me to my apartment house.

We went up to my apartment. I opened the door and stood to one side. "Step right in, gentlemen," I said, and switched on the lights.

They entered the place, then suddenly stopped.

"What the hell!" Sellers said.

"What's wrong?" I asked.

They stood to one side so I could see the interior of the apartment.

"Good heavens, somebody has wrecked the place!" I exclaimed.

Sellers and Giddings exchanged glances.

I hurried past them over to the desk and surveyed the jimmied lock with lugubrious resignation.

"Well, it's gone," I said.

Sellers shook his head. "This time you've got to come up with something better than that, Pint Size."

"What the hell do you mean, something better than that?" I blazed. "I've got some rights! Here's my place completely ruined and ransacked, and you birds are standing there dead on your feet. Just because I'm a private detective doesn't mean I have to put up with all *that* stuff! If you're talking about lawsuits, *I'll* file one.

"Now, suppose you quit kicking *me* around and find out who the hell ransacked this apartment."

Sellers looked at Giddings. "The guy's got a point," he said. "Let's get a fingerprint man up here and take a look."

Giddings gave a hollow, mocking laugh. "And waste *more* time?"

"We're laying a foundation," Sellers said.

He went to the phone and called headquarters.

By the time the fingerprint man arrived, I'd spotted the empty flask on the kitchen sink.

"That's not mine," I said.

"What isn't?"

"That flask."

"The guy may be right at that," Sellers said to Giddings. "He takes a drink with a babe once in a while, but he doesn't hit the booze. I'll bet he never has had a bottle in the apartment."

He turned to the fingerprint man. "Take a look."

The fingerprint man dusted the whiskey flask. "It's lousy with latents," he said.

"All right, let's get some photographs," Sellers said, "and let's take a look at Donald's fingerprints and make sure they aren't his."

They took my fingerprints; they dusted the apartment; they didn't find any fingerprints that weren't mine or the housekeeper's except the fingerprints on the whiskey flask.

"It looks like a plant," Giddings said.

"Of course it looks like a plant," Sellers told him, "but we aren't overlooking *any* bets; not in dealing with this guy. I'm telling you, he's smart."

"He *thinks* he's smart," Giddings sneered. "Wait until I get done with him."

"Come on, Pint Size," Sellers told me. "You're going up to headquarters."

"I believe we got enough prints on that flask to damn near make a classification," the fingerprint man said. "There are prints all over it."

I said, "The guys that picked on me were big fellows. I think I could identify one of them from a mug shot."

"Okay, Pint Size, we'll give you all the chance in the world," Sellers said.

It was shortly after 1:30 A.M. that I picked out a face in the mug shots.

"That looks like the guy," I told Giddings.

Giddings was skeptical. "Okay, Wise Guy," he said, "we'll check the fingerprints."

Ten minutes later there was a very great change in the manner of Inspector Thad Giddings.

"What about the prints?" I asked.

Giddings looked at me and shook his head wonderingly.

"They check," he said. "The guy's fingerprints are on that flask. Hell, you may be on the up and up."

I heaved a big sigh. "Well," I said, "now we know where the idol I had is."

"There are some other prints on there, too," Giddings said. "Let's not go off half-cocked on this."

"Have it your own way," I told them. "As far as I'm concerned, I'm a citizen whose apartment has been burglarized, and I'd like to see some police activity."

"You're getting it," Giddings told me. "You're getting it. Don't get ants in your pants."

They left me alone for twenty minutes; then Giddings and Frank Sellers both entered the room.

"I guess we've got your men identified, all right, Pint Size," Sellers said.

"How come?"

"The man you identified is named Ferguson. He's out on parole and he's living at 9611 Sixty-first Street. He makes regular reports to his parole officer, has got a good job working in a TV concern. He's an expert on electronics and has been making good on his parole.

"However, while he was in prison he was teamed up with a fellow named Jimmy Lenox who has the nickname of 'Next County' Lenox, because whenever anyone tried to pick him up for a job, he'd always swear he was in the next county at the time, and usually made it stick.

"Now then, the thing that gives you a break, Donald, is the fact that Jimmy Lenox's prints are also on that flask. That ties the two of them in together, and when those two crooks get together, you can gamble something is happening.

"Moreover, that address at 9611 Sixty-first Street almost backs up on the place where Mortimer Jasper is living on Carrolton Drive. Now then, we just *could* have something here."

I nodded.

"It'd be a good idea, under the circumstances, if you signed a complaint charging Lenox and Ferguson with burglary, and made an affidavit that would enable us to get a search warrant."

"Why should I sign anything?" I said. "Why don't you fellows take it on your own shoulders?"

"Now look, Donald," Sellers said, and his voice was almost pleading, "we're in deep enough on this thing. We've gone along on your say-so and…well, the whole thing is getting mixed up all to hell. We'd like to solve it, but we aren't going to stick our necks out any farther. Now, you're a private citizen as well as a private detective. Your place has been burglarized and you think you know the men who did it. Be a sport. Sign a complaint and an affidavit and let us use a search warrant."

I looked at Giddings. "I don't know whether I feel like cooperating or not. I've been kicked around too much this evening."

"Now, don't hold anything up against Thad," Sellers said. "Thad is just a good, two-fisted, square-shooting cop that maybe got you wrong earlier in the evening."

"I haven't heard him say so," I said.

Giddings took a deep breath. "Maybe I got you wrong earlier in the evening, Lam," he said.

The way he said it was like having all his teeth pulled.

"Come on," I told them, "let's go."

Chapter Twenty-One

It was two-thirty when the police cars slid up on the place at 9611 Sixty-first Street.

They did it in the most approved manner. They shut off the motors a block away and coasted up to the place. They used the emergency brakes to stop so the red brake light didn't give forth a telltale glare. They got out without the slamming of car doors. They had a sledge hammer and a couple of curved bars to jimmy doors fast. One detail went around to the back of the house, and Sellers and Thad Giddings went to the front.

After they'd been ringing the doorbell for a couple of minutes, a light came on inside the house and somebody inside the door said, "Who is it?"

"Police," Sellers said. "We have a search warrant. Open up."

"Hell, you've got nothing on us," the voice said.

"Open up. We have a warrant," Sellers said.

"You can't have a warrant," the voice said. "I haven't done anything."

"Open the door or we'll break it down," Sellers told him.

The door opened.

The tall man was standing there in athletic underwear and he was big. He even loomed half a head above Sellers.

Giddings pushed me forward. "Ever see this guy before?" Sellers asked, directing a flashlight on the top of the porch so that both of our features were illuminated in a bounce light.

"I never saw the guy before in my life," the big man said, "and I don't intend to be rousted out at this hour of the night to answer questions. You guys can go roll your hoops. I'm clean, and—"

"Who says you're clean?" Sellers interrupted. "Is this the guy, Donald?"

"That's the guy," I said, with conviction.

"I never saw that little sonofabitch in my life," the big man protested.

"Okay, Ferguson," Sellers told him, "we're coming in. We've got a warrant. Who else is in here with you?"

"No one."

About that time there was a commotion at the back and one of the men who had been detailed to watch the back door came in with a shorter individual who was wearing pants, shoes, coat and undershirt. He hadn't even stopped to put on a shirt.

"We caught this guy taking a sneak out the back," the officer said. "Look what he had in his coat pocket."

He held out a green jade Buddha with a flaming red ruby in the forehead.

The big man in the underwear cursed and tried to turn and run.

Sellers clipped him on the back of the neck.

The guy went down so hard I could feel the house shake.

"Come on," Sellers said, "move in. We're taking the joint to pieces."

Chapter Twenty-Two

My wristwatch said it was a little after four. The idea of going to my apartment was a physical torture. I thought of the mattress that had to be lifted down and put in place; the bed that had to be made; the knowledge that Bertha would be certain to be calling on the telephone at least by eight o'clock in the morning. It was all too much of a chore just to get a few hours' sleep.

I thought of Phyllis waiting. She'd have to wait.

I called a taxi and went to a Turkish bath, managed to get my clothes off, wrap up in a sheet and then limped down to the hot room.

It was a heavenly sensation to relax in the warm air and feel my muscles slowly soaking up the warmth and giving up the pain.

The attendant, who had been putting cold wet towels around the top of my head, came in with a glass of water and said, "There's a cop outside wants to see you; says his name is Sellers."

"Tell him to come in."

"He can't come in. He's dressed. He'd be sweating buckets inside of five minutes."

"Tell him I can't go out. I'd catch cold."

The attendant went away.

Within about five minutes, Frank Sellers came in, mad all the way through.

"Listen, Pint Size," he said, "who the hell do you think you're standing up?"

He took off his coat and necktie and threw them on a chair.

"I'm not standing up anyone," I said. "I just want to get some of the pain out of my muscles, and I'm not going out in the cold to talk with you. Now, what is it you want to know?"

"Now, look. Pint Size," Sellers said, "you've pulled a couple of mighty fast ones. I don't know how the hell you did it, and I'm not going to try to find out because we're sitting pretty. We got that safe open and we've got confessions out of Ferguson and Jimmy Lenox. Mortimer Jasper has been one of the biggest fences in the country, operating with a choice clientele, picking up only the stuff for which he had a customer in advance, and operating right under our noses without our even suspecting what was going on.

"I'll forgive you a lot for that. But I have an idea you may be a paragraph ahead of us on the murder.

"Now, that's in my department. I can't afford to come a cropper on that. I want to know what you know, and then I'm going away and leave you alone."

I said, "You're too opinionated to have an open mind on that murder."

"No, I'm not," he said. "But I'll tell you one thing. The only place from which that dart could have been fired was Phyllis Crockett's studio. The only time it could have been fired was while Phyllis Crockett and Sylvia Hadley were in there together —and Sylvia Hadley saw the tip of that blowgun as Phyllis Crockett was aiming it from the bathroom….You can get a first-degree murder conviction on that kind of evidence."

"Can you?" I asked.

Sellers started to sweat. He pulled a handkerchief from his hip pocket and mopped his forehead. "Damn it," he said, "don't argue with me. Tell me what you know, and let me get the hell out of here."

"Your premises are cockeyed," I said.

"What do you mean?"

"You say that the only place the dart could have been fired from was Phyllis Crockett's studio."

"Well? What's wrong with that?"

"Everything. The dart *couldn't* have been fired from the studio."

"You're nuts, Donald," Sellers said angrily. "We took that damn blowgun and stood it up there in that closet, and there isn't a single damn place where you can stand—even leaning out of the window so far as you can lean—and shoot a dart from that blowgun that would have landed in Crockett's chest—the one that was stuck in the wood up on top, I'll agree with you, *might* have been fired by someone standing by the window in the closet. But even so, a person would have had difficulty manipulating that blowgun—that's a five-foot, four-inch blowgun and—"

"What kind of rifling marks does it have?" I asked.

"What do you mean, rifling marks?" Sellers asked.

"So you can call in your ballistics department," I said. "You know, the way you do with a bullet. You identify the bullet that came from the gun by comparing the rifling marks and the grooves and the lands and the pitch and the marks of striation, and—"

"You're nuts," Sellers interrupted. "There aren't any grooves in a blowgun."

"You look here, Frank Sellers," I said, "do you mean to stand there and tell me that you can't tell from the marks on a dart that it was fired from a particular blowgun?"

"Of course not."

"Then," I said, "how in hell do you know the darts were fired from Crockett's blowgun?"

Sellers looked at me, started to say something, changed his mind, grabbed his handkerchief, mopped his forehead, ran the handkerchief around the collar of his shirt, looked at me again and said, "Sonofabitch!"

"How do you know they came from that blowgun?" I repeated.

"We don't," Sellers said after a minute.

"Well," I said, "*that* opens up an interesting possibility."

"Now, wait a minute, Donald. It stands to reason they had to come through that blowgun."

"Why does it stand to reason?"

"Well, blowguns aren't manufactured in mass production. Each one is an individual job in itself. Darts are made to fit a particular blowgun. Those are the darts that came with the blowgun. They're the ones that Crockett brought from Borneo. They've been seen in his collection. There's not much opportunity of confusing those darts with any others."

"Therefore you feel they had to be fired from that blowgun?"

"Sure."

"Why?"

"Because they were made to fit the blowgun."

"Then," I said, "if darts were made to fit a blowgun, it should be possible to make a blowgun to fit the darts."

Sellers wiped his hands with a handkerchief, ran it over his forehead and around his neck, and said, "Damn it. I've got to get out of here."

"What's holding you back?" I asked.

"You are."

"How come?"

"You're not telling me what you know."

"I'm simply asking you questions about blowguns."

"All right," he said, "go ahead and ask me questions. But those darts were fired from that blowgun. They had to be. I don't care what you say."

"You're certain?"

"Of course, I'm certain."

"That dart," I said, "that was embedded in the wood in that closet went in pretty deep."

"That's right. It went in pretty deep."

"You think Mrs. Crockett blew it from across the air well in that apartment house?"

"She had to. It was the only place it could have come from. You take the angle of that and it points right back to the bathroom window. There was no other place it could possibly have come from."

"Well," I said, "before you rule out the impossibilities, you should consider the possibilities. Now, have you taken one of those darts and tried blowing it through that blowgun and see how deep *you* can penetrate the wood with the dart?"

"Why should I?"

"It might be a good test."

"The wood is there, the dart is there. The dart was in the wood. You can't argue that away, Pint Size."

"I'm not trying to argue it away," I said. "All I'm telling you is that I don't think Phyllis Crockett could possibly have blown that dart that distance and had it stick in that wood that deep. I don't think *you* can take that dart and that blowgun and blow it into a piece of wood from a distance of even three or four feet and have it penetrate that deep."

"*Now* what are you getting at?" he asked, his manner showing his irritation.

"Now," I said, "I'm getting at the fact that simply because you saw a blowgun that was made to shoot darts, and saw a dart that was made to be shot from a blowgun, you jump to the obvious conclusion that the dart had to come from that blowgun. I don't think it came from any blowgun."

"Then where do you think it came from, if you're so damn

smart," Sellers asked, wiping the perspiration from his face and neck. "And quit running me around in circles because I'm going to get the hell out of here."

"Get the hell out any time you want to," I said, "but my own idea is that somebody manufactured a short-barreled weapon that worked with a charge of compressed air; that that person stood in the closet right next to Dean Crockett and fired the dart into his chest. Then *after* Dean Crockett fell, this person fitted the second dart into the mechanism and released it with a charge of compressed air so that it went into that piece of wood at an angle to make it appear that it had been fired from the bathroom window across the air well.

"And I think that person made a fatal mistake in a perfectly planned crime by not taking into consideration the fact that the compressed air in his gun generated more power than could possibly be generated with a pair of human lungs.

"As soon as I saw the setup, I felt absolutely certain that that dart in the wood had been the *second* dart that was fired instead of the *first*.

"You can reason it out," I said. "Put yourself in the position of Dean Crockett. If he had been standing there in the window and someone had fired a dart at him and had missed, and the dart had thudded into the wood, he would hardly have turned to face the window, put his hands on the window sill and exhibited a perfect target for the second shot. Remember, the guy had been around the jungles and he wasn't born yesterday.

"And when I saw that dart buried clean to the hilt in that hard wood, I knew damn well you couldn't have fired it in there with a blowgun."

I settled back and closed my eyes.

Sellers went to the door and bellowed at the attendant, "Hey, for God's sake, bring me a towel."

He came back and stood looking down at me with his feet spread wide apart, mopping away at his perspiring face, neck and hands with the towel. Then suddenly he wadded the towel up in a ball, slammed it down to the floor hard, picked up his coat, turned and walked toward the door without a word.

He got as far as the door, then turned on his heel. "All right, who did it?" he asked.

"Try the person who last saw him alive," I said, and closed my eyes. "I think they teach rookies that as the first procedure, don't they?"

Sellers stood there for a moment, then I heard the swinging doors as he went out, then he came back and said, "If it wasn't so hot in here that I don't dare to exert myself, I'd kick you right in that sassy fanny of yours. As it is, thanks for the information."

Chapter Twenty-Three

I got into the office about ten-thirty. I looked a little better, but I had a good shiner on the right side, I couldn't take a deep breath without it hurting, and I favored one side when I walked.

Elsie Brand came running out to meet me. "Bertha has to see you *just* as soon as you come in," she said. "She's been having kittens trying to locate you."

"Tell her I'm in," I said.

I eased myself down into the swivel chair and Bertha came barging in before I had settled back in a comfortable position.

"Frank Sellers is in my office," she said. "Can you come in?"

"Tell him to come in here."

"He won't like it."

"Tell him to come in here."

Bertha said, "You can't order cops around this way. We have to keep on the good side—"

I eased my aching frame in the swivel chair and closed my eyes. "It's okay," I said. "If he wants to see me, he can see me. If he doesn't, it isn't important. Tell him I've told him all I know."

Bertha strode out of the office.

In about ten seconds she was back with Frank Sellers. "How you feeling, Pint Size?" Sellers asked. His voice was friendly, almost respectful.

"Like hell."

"You sure took a beating."

"You aren't telling me anything."

Sellers seemed a little uneasy. "Donald," he said, "I wrapped that murder case up this morning."

"Crockett?"

"Crockett."

"Who did it?"

"Olney," Sellers said. "He was pretty damn slick about it. He made arrangements so that he could get the blowgun out of there without anyone knowing it. He carefully hollowed out the handle of the club flag, then he stole the darts and everything was set to plant the gun in Mrs. Crockett's studio. Of course, you butted in and saved him the trouble."

I changed my position slightly, trying to ease the pain in my side. "Made himself a little blowgun?" I asked.

"Nothing to it," Sellers said. "The tube wasn't over ten inches long, but he screwed one of those containers that holds compressed carbon dioxide on the end of it and worked out a trigger arrangement that sent the darts so fast and so hard that they were traveling like a bullet."

"Uh-huh."

"He'd been managing Crockett's business and his tax matters, and what with one thing and another, he'd got into Crockett to the tune of about eighty thousand bucks. Crockett was beginning to think something was wrong. Next he would have been having an audit made—or Olney thought that would be the next step."

I said, "That's nice. I was a little afraid he might have had his eye on Phyllis and wanted Crockett out of the way for that reason."

"Well, that's all there was to it," Sellers said. "Once we got on the right track it was easy. We searched his room. The damn fool hadn't even disposed of the air gun he'd manufactured."

I yawned. "Why did you come over here, Frank?"

"I wanted to talk with you before the case broke in the newspapers," Sellers said uncomfortably.

"Why?"

"Well," he said, "they'll probably interview you and I wondered what you were going to tell them."

"Me!" I said, raising my eyebrows. "Why, hell. I'm not going to tell them anything except that it was my privilege to work with Sergeant Sellers of Homicide last night while he was solving the theft of the jade Buddhas from the Crockett penthouse, that after he had solved that theft, Sellers went ahead on his own with cleaning up the Crockett murder case."

"What about our conference in the Turkish bath?" Sellers asked.

"What Turkish bath?" I asked.

All of a sudden Sellers reached down, grabbed my hand and started shaking it. "You're a game little bastard," he said, "and a damn good friend. There are times when I feel like I could kiss you—despite the fact that I know damn well you pulled some kind of a slick razzle-dazzle on us over those two idols, and, by God, Donald, I'm not sharp enough to find out what it was."

"Then why try?" I asked.

Sellers shook hands with me again, then suddenly grabbed Bertha and kissed her.

"You're the kind of private detectives we need in the city," he said, and walked out.

Bertha Cool stood there blinking her greedy little eyes at me.

"Well?" I asked.

I thought she wanted to ask about the fee in the Crockett case and what arrangements I'd made with Phyllis. But, instead of that, Bertha reached up and patted her lips.

"The sonofabitch kissed me," she said, tenderly.

You never can tell about women.